T

THOMAS JOSEPH BECK

To Save a Soul

WITHOUT WINGS BOOK 1

publishing

To Save a Soul, Without Wings, Book 1

For more information, email all inquiries to:
thomasbeck1122@gmail.com
Published by TJB Publishing (2021)

soulwithoutwings.com

Printed in the United States of America
ISBN-13: 978-1-7368974-0-9

Second Edition

TO SAVE A
SOUL

Without Wings Series

Thomas Joseph Beck

To Save A Soul

PROLOGUE

Truth called another meeting of her sister angels. Those human beings were in trouble again, and this time even Mother Earth herself was disappointed in them. She felt humankind had become a hopeless cause and it seemed the angels themselves had run out of ideas. Now, as the angels gathered in the auditorium, bells rang out, the stars blinked, and the universe itself twisted ever so slightly. Then a moment of silence.

Faith burst into the room franticly, disturbing the stillness. "Nicky Vocci is dead!" she yelled breathlessly as she threw open the heavy doors. The other angels looked at each other in confusion. "It's not Nicki Vocci's time," she explained. "His expiration date is still thirty years away." Faith took a deep breath and calmed herself. "Obviously, I can't make the meeting. I've got to sort this out. Sorry, ladies."

As the auditorium door shut behind her, the other angels stirred uncomfortably. Things like this didn't happen. What was going on?

From the front of the room, Truth turned to face the stunned gathering. "Ok, girls, everyone relax. It's going to be all right".

"What's happening, Truth?" asked Hope.

"Well," Truth started with a slow grin, "I think love did for us what we could not do for ourselves."

And so it began...

Knick Knack, Chips, and The Hump

The fishing boats lined up like warships.

"Get yer blues here!" the fishermen yelled from every dock, each trying to sell the day's catch. The sun thawed the earth as it awoke from a long winter's nap. It was springtime in Sheepshead Bay, Brooklyn. Nicky drove his brand-new 1973 Cadillac El Dorado down Emmons Avenue. This was his neighborhood — or as Nicky and his friends called it — their "territory" and it ran from Old Mill Basin to Coney Island. It was a vast area that was home to many diverse ethnic groups. Old Mill Basin, where the three friends lived, was largely a middle-class Italian neighborhood that ended at King's Highway.

On the other side were Marine Park and Gerritsen Beach, both predominantly Irish neighborhoods. If you went down Knapp Street toward the Belt Parkway and made a right, you were on Emmons Avenue, which resembled a small fishing village at the end of New York City.

Sheepshead Bay was also Italian. You could follow Emmons Avenue, make a left onto Ocean Parkway, and you'd be in Coney Island and the Brooklyn Aquarium. When you finished looking at the whales, you could ride the Cyclone and then go have one of the world's greatest hot dogs for lunch at Nathan's, one of Brooklyn's proud landmarks. Some say the egg cream, an invigorating drink made with chocolate or vanilla cream and seltzer, was invented here. The egg cream doesn't have egg in it, but on a hot summer's day, who cared? Unfortunately, Coney Island was the poorest of neighborhoods.

Nicky made a left onto Bedford Avenue. He drove past one of his favorite bars, Captain Quarter's. Brooklyn College was at the end of Bedford Avenue and, on Thursdays, all the nice, pretty Jewish girls from Brooklyn College would come for Ladies Night. Nicky and the boys joked that if you couldn't get laid in Quarter's on a Thursday night, you were either a priest or a fag.

Bedford Avenue looked like a historical destination. Huge oak trees lined the streets in front of all the Victorian-style homes. It was as if you were suddenly transported back to the South before the Civil War. Affluent Jewish families lived there: doctors, lawyers, and bankers. Their children went to college so they could become "somebody." The girls went to college, met future doctors or lawyers, and married them. This was their cultural heritage. But Thursday night was their chance for a brief escape. They'd put on tight bell-bottoms or miniskirts and head down to Sheepshead Bay and Captain Quarter's. They were going to "the other side" where the middle class lived. Quarter's hosted various groups of people: the fishermen who worked the boats, garbage men, transit workers from the depots in Coney Island, wannabe wiseguys, and even the real wiseguys. Normally it was a volatile place, like a volcano waiting to erupt. But on Thursday nights it was different. Everyone had gotten paid for a long, hard workweek and it was time to party, blow off some steam, maybe meet one of the "nice Jewish girls" and buy her a drink, maybe shoot a game of pool. And—if you got lucky—she'd put out. For those young ladies who did, the next day they'd blame the booze. And life carried on.

The Godfather was the movie to see at the time. Some of the young Italian men in the neighborhood acted as if they were in the Corleone family but not Knick Knack, Chips, and the Hump. They were already in a family—the Capozzoli family—and if you wanted to stay healthy, the Capozzoli family didn't exist. That was the unspoken rule. You were either in or you'd be told to "mind your own business."

Everyone in the family had a nickname. Nicky Vocci, Steve Dimarzo, and Sal Capozzoli were known as Knick Knack, Chips, and the Hump. The names sounded like adorable characters from a children's book rather than the vicious psychopaths they really were. They were the underworld's urban royalty and ruled their territory with quiet but deadly intimidation and murder. They had money and power and, for the past ten years, they'd been on a fast track.

It all started back in the summer of 1963 with a cop named Gilinski. Big Al Gilinski was a football hero back in the forties. He'd played fullback for Madison High School and won a full scholarship to Michigan State University. But in the spring of '46, Al's father died of a heart attack. Al gave up football and stayed home to take care of his mother and three sisters. Three years later, Al graduated from the police academy and became a cop. He was six foot six, 240 pounds, with dark,

9

thick hair and dark eyes. His face showed a hint of humor on a surface that was hard as a rock. Al was also a closet intellectual and became an expert in the study of the humanities and social science. The streets of New York City were his classrooms.

In 1954, Al was made the youngest detective in the NYPD—and the biggest thorn in Salvatore Capozzoli's side. The newspapers dubbed their continuing conflict "Big Al vs. Big Sal." Everyone was amused, except Al and Sal. After nine years of this, Salvatore Capozzoli's right-hand man, Joey Vocci, aka Joey V, had had enough. Al had just sent some of the family's best soldiers, two judges, plus an assortment of cops who were on the payroll to jail. It was time for the cop to go, and on a summer morning in July of 1963, Joey V lay in wait outside of the Gilinski home. When the big cop came out to get in his car, Joey V sprang into action. He ran at him, firing his gun. Al, ever the athlete, displayed some acrobatic moves and shot Joey V dead.

The morning after his father's funeral, 15-year-old Nicky Vocci stood on the beach at Coney Island, watching the sunrise against the surf. He played the tape of the proceedings over and over again in his head. He saw all the wiseguys talking about how much they respected his father. Salvatore Capozzoli, the don himself, gave the eulogy. Oh, they put on quite a show. You might even have thought they really cared. But behind all those accolades, Nicky realized no one was going to do anything. Al Gilinski got a medal. The papers called him a hero. "New York City's bravest son," one newspaper wrote. He was on the nightly news constantly. Some famous biographer had even announced that he wanted to write the story of Al's life as the hero cop and family man who took care of his mother and helped raise his sisters.

Nicky's father, however, was the gangster who got what he deserved. Don Capozzoli would have had nothing if it weren't for Nicky's father. Despite this, the don would do nothing to avenge his death. The family was just a bunch of fair-weather friends who performed ludicrous rituals that didn't mean anything. The family was really just all about money and power and not getting caught.

Nicky learned the most important lesson of his life from this event: Don Capozzoli was smart. The don would think and plan, while Joey V just reacted. And that murderous temper had gotten him killed. Don Capozzoli had used his father's merciless demeanor to get to the top. And now, with a tear in his eye, he said that his hands were tied. He couldn't take revenge on a hero cop.

Nicky had taken a lot of beatings from his father. He knew he was an animal. But still, he was his father, and Nicky was going to avenge his father's death. He was gonna kill that cop, join the family, and work his way to the top. He was gonna watch and learn. But first he had to kill the cop and get away with it. He knew that the thing he had going for him was his age. No one would suspect a teenager like him. He had to think. No detail could be left out; nothing could be taken for granted. He would have to learn Al Gilinski's habits. Everyone had a routine, and that meant anyone could be killed. Nicky just had to wait until the time was right; he knew that Chips and the Hump always had his back.

Nicky lit a cigarette. *I'm coming, dirtbag.*

❖

Nicky was sitting in an enormous school auditorium. There was a vacant stage in front of a large movie screen. He looked around. "Yo!" he called out.

Nothing.

He yelled out again, louder this time. "Yo! What the hell? Anybody here?"

Still nothing.

"Stop this!" He stood up and started to leave as the room around him began to sparkle. He sat back down. It was so wonderful.

How is this happening? he thought. He stood up again in the awe-inspiring room, his mood carefree. Suddenly, luminous energy enveloped him. He was driven back into his seat. He tried to scream, but nothing came out. His mind raced. *I can't move! Get off me! Oh, shit, what is this? Help me! Help! Oh God, please...*

Silence.

The sound of his heartbeat was all he could hear. It was deafening. It pounded, faster and faster. Boom, boom, boom. *I'm gonna die!* The thought became paramount in his mind. He grabbed his chest. It's gonna blow! Utter stillness fell upon him as he was cast into darkness. He sat, terrified, trying to calm down. His mind was blank, he couldn't move, and sweat poured out of him.

From behind him, there came a sound.

"Oh man, what the hell now?" he shouted. He listened hard. *Could that be the flutter of wings?* "Yes, it's wings," he said aloud. A thought crossed his mind. *Bats. They fly in the dark. If it's bats, what the hell are they doing here?* Then he changed his mind. *No, it's a flock of birds. What kind of birds fly in the dark? Oh, shit, what is this?*

He realized they were coming toward him. He leaped to his feet and faced the sound. Something whizzed past him. A giant wing grazed the side of his head.

Nicky sat up with a start. "What the hell!" he said startled.

He flinched as the doorbell rang. His sweaty skin stuck to the plastic covers of his mother's plush gold velour couch. He knew he'd been dreaming; yet he felt apprehensive. The doorbell rang again and again.

"Wait a freakin' second," he yelled at the front door. He suddenly remembered that when he'd gotten home from the beach, he'd laid down on the living room sofa for a nap.

The doorbell rang again. Nicky jumped to his feet, walked to the door, and swung it open in a rage. There stood the Hump and Steve Dimarzo, smirking.

"You were jerking off, weren't you?" said the Hump as Steve snickered.

"Shut up, you idiot," snarled Nicky, trying to shake the weird feeling of fear and confusion that lingered. He had no way of knowing the dream would recur for the rest of his life. As the years passed, the dream came more frequently and Nicky developed a fear of birds. It was always the same in every dream, and Nicky always woke up terrified.

The three boys stood in the basement. Each took a turn holding the .38-caliber revolver that once belonged to Joey V. Nicky wanted to kill Officer Al Gilinski and become a made man within the Capozzoli family. He had a plan to enact once he was in the family that would give him his own crew in five years. To succeed, he wanted and needed his friends' help.

It would all start with the death of Gilinski. Steve and the Hump said they were in. It was there, in the basement, that the boys swore an alliance with each other—a vow each would keep forever. They hadn't a clue that their fathers had done the exact same thing years before. The boys entered into an association for mutual benefit. Now they had to successfully kill Gilinski.

Al Gilinski was on top of the world. He felt like Superman. The attention was seductive and he loved being a hero. His peers were concerned for his safety. Joey V had been an important big-time mobster. Al ignored their warnings, saying he'd put the next punk in a box, too.

That August, he was back on the six and eleven o'clock news. He was telling the city of New York his story. He told anybody watching he and his partner owned a cabin upstate and that in late October and early November, they always went to the Catskills to hunt. The boys happened to be watching the news that night. The three boys grinned at each other while sitting on Nicky's mother's sofa.

"We're gonna find that cabin," Nicky said.

"It's a done deal," agreed Steve as they all started snickering and snorting like hyenas before a kill.

Later, the friends found the cabin. When the time came, they drove up ahead of Al and waited.

Al stumbled back and forth until he finally found his tree. Now came the hard part. He put his foot on the tree peg and with his right hand, he reached up to grab another peg. As he struggled to pull himself up, a voice called out to him.

"Yo, Al."

That would be the last thing Al ever heard. A .38-caliber bullet found its way between his eyes.

Not too far away, Al's partner, Richie Kelly, leaped out of his tree stand. He'd heard someone yell and seen a flash and then a shot that shocked awake the predawn morning. Richie landed on his feet and ran in the direction of the commotion. In the sudden excitement, he'd forgotten his rifle. He ran faster and faster, calling out his partner's name.

Without warning, the Hump stepped out in front of him and punched him in the face. Richie's face exploded like a smashed tomato splattering blood all over the Hump. The well-delivered punch drove Richie's nose into his brain and he lay dead in the snow. The Hump threw the lifeless body over his shoulder and walked through the woods to a clearing where Steve Dimarzo waited with a stolen van. Steve slid open the door, and the Hump tossed in the body.

"Cool," Steve cooed.

"Shut up and start the van," said the Hump. Then he went back to help Nicky. With both bodies in the van, they headed for Billy Bundles' farm in Greenville.

Back in 1950, Nicky's father, Joey V, was serving a three to five year sentence in Sing Sing. He had a cellmate named Billy Franks. Franks was lanky with a whitish, almost albino, complexion. The blue of his eyes and the pale blond of his crew cut were the colors he possessed. He was a thief by trade and burglary was his specialty. He also boasted he had the greatest hideout in the world -- his grandmother had left him one hundred acres in the mountains upstate. It had only one road in, and no one could find it. Joey challenged him by asking him why he was sitting in a cell if it was all that great. Billy told him he'd gotten caught in a stolen car while racing through the town of Greenville on his way to the farm.

Not too bright, Joey thought. *I like that in a potential crew member.*

Billy was as dumb as a box of rocks, but he was funny. One day Billy told Joey V that he threw the stuff he stole but couldn't get rid of into a vat filled with hydrochloric acid. He kept the vat at the back of the farm and said it was fun to watch stuff dissolve.

Three years later, when they were released from prison, Billy took Joey to the farm and showed him the vat. In the fall of 1953, Joey V brought his first body to the farm. They dropped it in the vat. The body dissolved like Alka-Seltzer. From that day on, Billy had a job. He was an inept burglar no more. He picked up the Capozzoli family's not so dearly departed and made them disappear. No body, no crime. The family members would call Billy and tell him to come pick up a bundle. Soon he was known as Billy Bundles.

❖

It was 4:45 in the morning when the Hump knocked on Billy's door. Bundles answered the door to find the sons of Don Capozzoli, Joey V, and Louie Dimarzo were standing in front of him. He wondered how these kids had found him.

And it got worse. Not only had these teenagers invaded his farm, but they had also brought with them the bodies of two New York City police officers they claimed to have.

Billy started to panic and told them to leave. Nicky stuck the .38 between his eyes.

"Listen, whack job, either help us with these bodies or become one."

Billy started preparing the vat as the boys dumped the bodies on the barn floor. Nicky went through Al's pockets and found his badge.

"I've got a souvenir," he called out.

Billy told the boys he'd do the rest. He just wanted them to leave.

As they sped back to Brooklyn, the Hump said, "Hey, Nicky's got a knickknack." The boys all laughed. When they got home, Nicky put Al's badge in a cigar box. He would keep other souvenirs of the people he killed. By the time he died, he would have four cigar boxes, and he'd always be known as Knick Knack.

They sank the van at the beach when they arrived back in Brooklyn. They were all home and in bed by sunrise. It was early Sunday morning, and most of Brooklyn slept. No one had even realized they had been gone.

❖

Nicky got a phone call around one o'clock that afternoon. It was Don Capozzoli himself. He told Nicky to meet him and his son at the Lucky U which was owned by Steve Dimarzo's father, Louie. Louie was the family bookie and also in charge of laundering the family's money. He wasn't into the violent end of the family's business. Still, he was a key player. If Joey Vocci was the don's right-hand man, Louie Dimarzo was his left.

To Steve, his father was just an accountant, a man too weak for the real action. Steve thought being a mob soldier was the greatest job in the world, but Steve's father wanted him to go to college and make something of himself. Steve, of course, had other plans. He could steal a car in no time flat, and the family owned chop shops in Coney Island. Out of respect for his father, however, Steve was not allowed to do any kind of work for the family. Instead he was a bar back at his father's bar. He was expected to stay in school.

Steve was pissed. Why should he have to break his ass doing this little job and do well in school when the Hump and Nicky didn't have to? Steve's father told him to be his own man and not to worry about what Nicky or the Hump did or didn't do.

"Besides, you're smarter than them," his dad would say.

Steve kept quiet and smiled after each lecture, but he always thought to himself, *F you*. Steve felt his father wanted him to become a pussy. But that afternoon, Steve Dimarzo's life would change forever.

❖

The Lucky U was located on Avenue U and Herring Street. Avenue U ran from east to west in Brooklyn. With its busses and trains, you could get to any borough in the city. So it was on Avenue U that all the neighborhoods came together. People shopped and caught trains into Manhattan there. It was an artery in Brooklyn—a neutral one for all the different ethnic backgrounds. No matter what neighborhood you were from, if you needed anything from clothes to food or an ice-cold glass of beer, you went to Avenue U.

In 1946, Louie Dimarzo opened the Lucky U. He bought the two storefronts on the corner and blackened the windows of one of them. Then he took out the front door and made a wall. This was the back room of the Lucky U. Wiseguys from all over the city would go there to drink and gamble. The cops were paid to look the other way. Don Capozzoli's office was there, too. In the back of the back room, all Capozzoli family matters were discussed.

The other storefront became the neighborhood bar. The Lucky U was like all bars of its time—a long mahogany bar with stools lined up in front of it. Reingold and Sheaffer were on tap. There was a cash register, an assortment of liquor bottles, and a great mirror that ran the length of the bar, so you could watch yourself get drunk. The Lucky U seemed like every other neighborhood bar, with one exception: no one from the neighborhood ever dared go in there. It was as if the bar itself didn't exist.

Word got around to the Capozzoli family to stay away from the Lucky U until 3:00 p.m. because the don had personal business to discuss. It seemed that his son and Nicky had killed Al Gilinski and another cop, and their partner, Steve Dimarzo, had stolen a van and driven them. Billy Bundles assured the don that the bodies were gone. No one even suspected they were missing. By the time they did, the cops would have no evidence. The don wished he had thought of this. It was perfect —who would suspect two fifteen-year-old boys? But now the don had to make sure that Billy Bundles and Louie Dimarzo were the only ones who knew what the boys had done. Nicky and the Hump were gonna become made. Steve Dimarzo was going to military school. His father said he had no choice.

Louie Dimarzo beat his son Steve with a belt then dragged the hurt, angry teenager to the Lucky U. Louie was so mad he could chew nails. His son was gonna do something with his life if it killed him. They arrived at noon. Louie had to go out collecting gambling debts.

"While I'm gone, clean up this place," he told Steve.

Steve was mopping behind the bar when the front door swung open. In walked Joey Filppo, a potato chip vendor. The kids in the neighborhood would wave as he drove his blue-and-white Wise truck through the streets. Filppo was a tall, flimsy man with an aggressive nature. He claimed he'd had the Jets in a football pool; Steve's father said he hadn't. They argued about it all week. On this Sunday afternoon, Filppo was determined to get his money.

When he saw Steve behind the bar with a mop, he figured he'd scare him and started shouting at him.

"Where's your deadbeat father, you little puke?"

In response to the remark, Steve broke a bottle of Jack Daniel's over the vendor's head. Then he grabbed a baseball bat, leaped over the bar, and beat Joey Filppo to death. The front door opened, and there stood Don Capozzoli, the Hump, and Knick Knack.

"What the —— is wrong with you kids? Close that door and lock it!" the Don yelled.

Steve stood over Joey Filppo's body, covered in blood.

"He called my father a deadbeat. F—— him and his family," Steve said.

The Don started laughing. "From now on, I'm calling you Chips. Get it? Chips," he said, smiling. The boys started to laugh.

"Okay," the Don said, "Get that body in the basement. Sal, move your fat hump ass." (That's right; his own father gave him the name "the Hump.") The Hump dragged the body downstairs while Nicky and Chips mopped up the blood. When Louie returned and saw what his boy had done, he was heartsick. Who was this animal he called his son?

The Lucky U never opened that day. Billy Bundles drove down from upstate. That night around 1:00 a.m., the bar was burned down. Steve Dimarzo was now known as Chips. Something had happened to him as he crushed Joey Filppo's bones with the bat. As the man cried for mercy, Steve Dimarzo had gotten an erection. As Chips, he would become the deadliest of the three. He loved killing; to him it was better than sex. He would spend the rest of his life doing a lot of both.

On Monday morning, Louie Dimarzo, his wife, Joann, and their daughter, Marie, got on a plane headed for Italy at JFK airport. They would never return to America. Chips never saw or spoke to them again.

For forty years, the cops and FBI would try to find out what happened to Al Gilinski and Richie Kelly. They knew it was a mob hit, but knowing and proving are two different things. No one suspected Joey V's son, Nicky. They just figured he was too young.

Knick Knack's Plan

• Kill Al Gilinski (revenge for father); build reputation.

• Get into a powerful earning crew. Watch the head of the crew, learn what he knows. Become better friends with his friends. Earn the most money for my crew. When leader of crew trusts me, kill him and take his crew.

• In order for plan to work, I must convince Don Capozzoli that I could do more, earn more, for him.

• Marcus Walker, aka Black, is the leader of the Black Knights in Coney Island. He runs drugs in and out of Sheepshead Bay, Brighton Beach, and part of Rockaway. Frances O'Trey runs the Irish gang the Beach Rats, who supply drugs for Marine Park, Gerritsen Beach, and the Nostrand projects. Form an alliance; work with the Irish and blacks. Seek more power in numbers. Don't just do business with the Italians.

• Become so powerful not even Don Capozzoli can stop me. Get rich, then get out. Disappear by the time I'm fifty.

❖

There stood Lisa Stein outside Sheepshead Bay High School. It was springtime 1973, and she was waiting for her boyfriend, Knick Knack Vocci. Everyone treated her differently now. They took her seriously.

She met Nicky a little over a year before when her best friend (and older cousin), Debbie, who was a freshman at Brooklyn College, got a phony ID for her. The two young girls went off to ladies' night at Captain Walters. Lisa was waiting for a drink at the bar. The place was packed. She noticed a

22

booth in the back, and although there was barely any standing room at all, nobody was sitting in that booth. Lisa got her drink and headed for the empty booth. Everyone stopped and stared as she sat down. Debbie came running up to her. "Don't sit there!" she yelled.

Just then a big, hard-faced thug walked past her. He was tall, with huge hands. He had thick black hair and green eyes. Lisa thought to herself, *you are trouble, but man you are hot!* Lisa stood up and started out of the booth.

Nicky almost swallowed his tongue when he saw Lisa. She was five foot six with long, shapely legs. She wore her hair in a ponytail and had sparkling blue eyes and dimples. She even had a beauty mark on the corner of her full mouth.

"Hey, sit back down, you and your friend," Nicky said.

"Thank you, but we have to go," Debbie said.

"Oh, I'm sorry, I thought I said sit down," Nicky said.

Debbie sat across the table as Lisa and Nicky talked the night away. Nicky bought them drinks all night, and Lisa thought he was wonderful. Debbie, however, could not wait to get out of there. Around midnight, Nicky paid for their cab ride home.

On the way home, Lisa felt like Cinderella. She had met her prince. Debbie looked out the cab window. She was worried about Lisa. She had just wanted one wild night out, but instead her younger cousin had fallen for the devil. So much had happened since then. She tried to explain to her parents that she was going to be a model. They didn't understand that Nicky was no ordinary twenty-five-year-old. He knew people —important people. He was going to get her modeling career off the ground. They were in love. She was going to see the world, not just stay in Brooklyn and get married to some schmuck doctor with a bunch of kids or waste her life away at school. The time to live was now, and she was going to do so. What hurt most of all was that Debbie couldn't see it either.

Debbie was on Lisa's parents' side. Lisa knew Debbie's attitude was really just jealousy. Debbie was still mad about the time she went on a date with Chips. After dinner and a movie, Chips parked his car in Marine Park. He tried to put his hand up Debbie's dress and wound up throwing her out of the car when she wouldn't let him. So now Nicky and his friends were animals. But Nicky wouldn't do that. He treated Lisa like a queen.

After all the fighting, Lisa left home and moved in with Nicky. Her parents sat Shiva for her.

Today Lisa was especially eager. Nicky had sent pictures of her to a friend of his. It turned out Nicky's friend loved what he saw, and now Lisa was off to Paris to start her modeling career. In reality, she would never see seventeen.

Nicky's mother moved to California shortly before his seventeenth birthday. She couldn't bear the thought of Nicky being like his father. She left him the house and everything in it. She emptied her bank accounts, got money from Don Capozzoli, and left Brooklyn with a million dollars—money she would gladly give up if she could have a good boy. But Nicky worked for the family now, so she had to go. She never stopped praying for him, though, and she died thinking God had ignored her prayers.

Nicky had been on his own for eight years. Six months ago, Lisa had moved in. He had found happiness, something he had never known. Their first night living together, Lisa grabbed one of Nicky's tank tops and put it on as a nightie. She approached Nicky as he lay in their bed. Before long, they had made love in every part of the house.

After her shower before going to sleep, Lisa would sit on the edge of the bed and Nicky would brush her long brown hair. With each gentle stroke, Lisa would move her head slightly and moan with pleasure. As the brush moved through her hair, the aromatic fragrance of just-washed skin and perfume would siege Nicky's senses. The love he felt was overwhelming as he fought back tears of happiness.

"I love you, Nicky," Lisa would whisper, and he would scoop her up in his arms. Then the two would fall back into the bed. Lisa would fall asleep in Nicky's arms, her head on his chest. Lisa called him Nickyboy because, as she told him, guys with "boy" at the end of their names turned her on. She was the only human who could get away with that. On the street, his name was Knick Knack, Nicky, or sir. He told her everything— even that he was afraid of birds. Nicky loved her. He wanted to crawl inside her until the world went away.

But on the outside, he had to act strong.

There was no room for love on the streets of Brooklyn. Because of this, the romance couldn't last. In Nicky's world, you had to be alert. His life was brutal, and to the people he knew, he was smart and sadistic. He had to be; after all, he had a plan, and right after Lisa moved in, it started to take shape.

Through Lisa, Nicky met a doctor named Seth Goldstein. He was a thin little man with a big bald head and bad breath. He resembled a Jewish troll. That didn't matter, though, because he had two things Nicky admired: balls and greed. The doctor, it turns out, could get his hands on endless supplies of prescription drugs. He just needed someone to get them out on the street. He was taking the risk, so he wanted 25 percent of the profits. Nicky knew this was his chance, so he set up a meeting in Manhattan. At the meeting would be Marcus Walker, aka Black, the head of the Black Knights of Coney Island; Frances O'Trey, the leader of the Irish gang the Beach Rats; the good Dr. Goldstein; and, of course, Nicky.

At that meeting, Nicky proposed a partnership. The Capozzoli family would offer police protection to the gangs. They would deal drugs throughout their territories, and then the Irish, Blacks, and Italians would split the profits. There would be enough money, and enough power, for everyone. Together they'd be unstoppable. They would rule Brooklyn.

Black loved the idea, but O'Trey didn't want to work with anybody but his own. The meeting ended in a stalemate. O'Trey wouldn't budge. Two weeks later, Frances O'Trey disappeared. His right-hand man, Jimmy Sullivan, aka Sullie, took over as head of the gang.

The deal went through, and the streets of Brooklyn from Coney Island to Old Mill Basin were infested with drugs. Don Capozzoli was so proud of Nicky and the boys that Nicky got to kill Paulie Stepfinao and take over his crew. Don't you just love it when a plan comes together?

Nicky yelled as he bounced off the bed and onto the floor. Lisa sat up and turned the lights on. She laughed as Nicky got to his feet.

"I'm sorry, baby. Are you okay?"

Nicky told her about the dream. He hadn't had it since she moved in. Just when he had thought it was over, it had come back—worse than ever. The auditorium was bigger, and this time it seemed as if an arm and a wing had grazed him. Birds and bats don't have arms.

Lisa sat up in bed, listening to Nicky ramble. She felt bad he had been sweating.

"Baby, come on back to bed." Nicky rolled up in a ball as she rocked him in her arms. She kissed his forehead. "You're not so tough."

As Lisa slept that night, Nicky stared into the bathroom mirror. He wondered what would happen if Lisa were sitting in a restaurant with Chip and the Hump, and she started talking about how cute he was. Even the don was calling him Jerry Lee, after Jerry Lee Lewis, who had married his fifteen-year-old cousin. When he'd called him Jerry Lee at his house the night before, Chips and the Hump both laughed. What if they found out about the nightmares, or that he was afraid of birds?

That can't happen, he thought, *no matter what.* He couldn't afford to look weak. What was he thinking? This had to stop. He couldn't have both love and power.

Rosie Frako was a prostitute the boys shared. She worked in one of the family's brothels. Nicky thought she was an Italian version of Lisa, but with big breasts. Nicky would pay her from time to time to keep an eye on Lisa—take her shopping et cetera. But now Nicky had another job for her—a very well paying job.

Nicky picked Lisa up and took her back to the house. When they got there, he carried her into the bedroom. Then he stripped her naked. The two made love over and over and over again.

"Go faster, you hump. Stop acting like a hump."

Before he knew it, he was known as the Hump. His father got a kick out of that. Nicky, however, called him Saldo; never once did he call him the Hump. And for that the Hump would die for Nicky. Everyone on the street knew you might get Nicky, but then you would have to deal with the Hump.

The Hump was a genius with numbers. After Chip's father went back to Italy, the don was amazed at how smart his son was. He put him to work on the family's money matters—a job he did better than Louie Dimarzo. Now the don was grooming the Hump for the day he would take over the family. What the don never realized was how much his son hated him. To the Hump, Nicky and Chips were his only family. All a boy wants is his father's love and approval. If he doesn't get it, he becomes an angry young man—and then an angry old man.

Chips was twenty-five years old, and there wasn't an ounce of fat on his well-proportioned frame. He looked like an elegant Hollywood leading man, not a psychotic street thug. Chips and Rosie pulled into the parking lot at JFK International Airport in Queens.

Back in Brooklyn, on King's Highway and Avenue U, the Hump walked to his truck. On his shoulder was a huge trunk, but to him it might as well have been a pillbox. He tossed it into the stolen Ford Bronco and drove toward Nicky's house. The Hump was also twenty-five years old. He had considerable size and strength. He did most of his killing with his bare hands. For him it was easier and less messy.

Back at JFK, Chips and Rosie were having an exasperating discussion. She wanted him to pull his pants up. He was trying to force her head in his lap, assuring her there was plenty of time before her flight left.

Lisa dried off, staring at herself in the mirror. She was going to be the best model Paris ever had. She felt she'd be queen of the runway. All of Paris would worship her. *Won't all the losers in Brooklyn be jealous?* And maybe if her parents apologized really nicely—okay, she'd make them beg—then and only then would she see them. But she was determined they were going to pay for the flight to Paris. Then she thought about what an animal she turned Nicky into. *He couldn't get enough.* She dropped her towel to the floor. *Let's see if he's got one more in him.* She opened the bathroom door and stepped into the bedroom. She didn't see Nickyboy come up behind her, but suddenly he was on her.

Lisa felt as if her eyes were going to pop out. *Air! Please, God, help me!* She winced, then saw only blackness. Nicky let go, and Lisa's body fell to the floor with a loud thump. Nicky got on his knees and held her.

"I'm sorry, babe, I'm sorry." Nicky held Lisa's body, rocking back and forth.

The doorbell rang, and Nicky let the Hump in. Up the stairs he climbed, with the trunk on his shoulder. He walked into the bedroom where Lisa's body was lying on its stomach.

"She's naked. You've been banging her all day," the Hump said.

At first Nicky didn't answer, but then he said, "I was saying good-bye."

"She had a great future," the Hump said, staring at her ass.

"Could you please just get rid of it?"

"Hey, you know what?"

"No, what?"

"Today she was coming and going."

They both shared a belly laugh, and with that, the Hump picked up Lisa's body. He dropped Lisa into the trunk the way one might toss a wet towel into a hamper.

On this spring day of 1973, Rosie flew to Paris not as herself but as Lisa in disguise. She'd check into George V as Lisa Stein and leave a suitcase filled with Lisa's clothes and Lisa's pocketbook in the room. Then Rosie would disappear in Europe. She would be paid $25,000 to take part in this dicey plan.

Now, as for the rest of it, that was easy. The Hump drove the body upstate to Billy Bundles. As far as anyone knew, Lisa went to Paris and never returned. As mentioned before—no body, no crime.

The projector stopped, and the lights came on. Nicky could hear the 8mm film reel spin to a stop. He was back in the school auditorium, but this time he watched an accurate account of an event that had happened over thirty years before. As he sat, he pondered how that could be. He stood up and faced the projection booth window.

"Yo, who's up there? I'm ready to wake up now!"

The exit doors to the left of the stage rattled. He heard what sounded like young girls giggling. He turned and faced the doors, but before he could say anything, they opened. In walked six female angels pushing a hospital gurney with a body on it covered by a sheet. Nicky sat down, his jaw hanging open. *Angels have wings and arms*, he thought.

"Okay, I'm ready to wake up now."

The angels giggled again.

"Wake up, Nick; wake up, Nick. Please, Nick, wake up!"

The angels broke out laughing. The smallest angel walked over to Nicky's row. She passed the empty seats and sat down next to him. Nicky sat in shock.

"Hello, Nicky. I'm the angel Faith. Welcome."

"Am I dead?"

"No, you're dreaming."

"Really? It seems so real."

"I lied. You're dead."

The other five angels roared in laughter.

"Is this heaven?"

"Sort of."

"What do you mean, 'sort of'?"

"You don't belong in heaven. Just one episode of your life showed that."

"So I'm going to hell. Or is this hell? Could you help me out of here?"

"Do you want to go to heaven?"

"Doesn't everyone?"

"Have I got a deal for you."

"What deal?"

"Let's start at the beginning."

In the Beginning

In the beginning there was Love. With a small flicker of light, Love took a deep breath and forced it out, and with a loud bang the universe was created. She gave birth to the planets and the stars. Love nestled into the center of the universe.

Love grew strong, and the universe spread out into an infinite circle. The spirit of the universe was created. This spirit of nature was that of love and knowledge. It would forever expand and create. And the spirit of the universe lined up all the planets and moons around the brightest stars. Then the spirit of the universe made energy that spanned the circle. And from all this came happiness that would enlarge and Love saw this and said that it was good.

The spirit of the universe was ever growing. Supernatural beings came to be. They were to attend to the spirit of the universe, which would teach them the ways of love. The spirit of the universe called them angels. These beings could take physical form, and when they did they were winged beings. But in order to keep balance, he made some of them passionate and some of them combative. There were twelve in all.

The passionate angels were Faith, Truth, Humility, Acceptance, Serenity, and Grace. Their essential natures were strong emotions that are deeply and sincerely felt. The combative angels were Pride, Anger, Suspicion, Fear, Lust, and Insecurity—their essential natures were the bold and energetic pursuit of one's ends—a relentless desire to dominate.

Faith was petite in stature. She had short blond hair and bright blue eyes, along with high cheekbones and dimples. She was childlike, for she knew complete trust. She displayed confidence and a great sense of humor, and she was devoted to teaching humankind to believe in hope.

Truth was tall, lean, and busty, with long, flowing brown hair and steady brown eyes. She had a veracity to see reality and was devoted to teaching humankind the application of integrity.

Grace had bouncy strawberry-blond hair and alluring green eyes. Her form was that of a dancer. She had an overwhelming capacity for mercy and was devoted to teaching humankind that the greatest charity is forgiveness.

Humility had charcoal eyes and ebony skin; her beauty was beyond any vanity. She knew the importance of a pure heart and was devoted to teaching mankind that modesty and unity are goals.

Acceptance had the appearance of a geisha girl. She had great strength, which she got from tolerance. She allowed what was to be to be. She was devoted to teaching humankind dignity and patience.

Serenity had long silvery hair and a round face that displayed wisdom. She had the highest form of tranquility and was devoted to teaching humankind that inner calmness is the path to peace.

Pride possessed a muscular physique and stone-cold eyes. That's what made this angel so attractive, but it was his self-glorification that made him foolish. Humankind could have learned satisfaction and joy but instead were taught arrogance.

Lust had the form of an obese man who never had enough of anything. He should have taught humankind of a drive or desire for life; instead, he taught addiction.

Suspicion was a long and lanky timid angel that thought something was always wrong. He reacted without proof, full of resentment and doubt.

Insecurity was a dwarf; always depressed, uncaring and tactless, self-centered to the extreme. He could have taught vulnerability to humankind in times of helplessness. Instead, mankind learned self-doubt, instability, and self-pity.

Fear, appearing tall and pale, a combative angel able to take many forms — a real chameleon. Humans listen to him most. He could have taught humankind how to thrive on earth. Instead, he wields cowardice and anxiety to teach them isolation and paranoia.

Anger was unapproachable yet alluring, ever able to enchant humanity with his destructive rush. He could have taught discipline and self-control instead of chaos.

The heart does not know it's an organ, one part of a whole human being, a key unit that sustains life, which was given to us as a gift. We all began with a sperm and an egg. We started as a cell, then became more cells, and as the cells came together, a heart, lungs, and other organs were formed. When we were born, all these parts made up the whole.

We are all individuals (meaning we are undivided), but still we are all the same. We were all given life so we could learn from one another. Together our purpose is to establish a focal consciousness with the spirit of the universe. We are each like a cell; however, together we are a species. We live on a planet. Mother Earth is an organ in the body of the universe, just as the heart is just one part of one whole human being.

In other words, we are all creations of Love. We are all spiritual beings having a human experience. Unlike the angels, we are subject to death, which means our only limitation is time. We have a beginning and an end, but only as we exist on this plane. The soul was created by Love; therefore, it never dies. It can be born again and again, and each time we come back, we learn more, and as the souls who are old learn more, they teach the souls who are new.

How does the soul learn? Each human soul is taught by one of the angels, and when you have come back enough times and learned enough, you move onto another plane. In other words, human beings are angels without wings.

TO SAVE A SOUL: PART 1

The lights came on again in the auditorium. The only sound was that of the reels spinning to a halt. Five angels were seated on the stage. Faith, the sixth angel, was sitting next to Nicky.

"I love that story. I can hear it over and over again without growing tired of it. So what do you think?" she asked Nicky.

"I'm not dreaming, am I?"

Faith yelled up to the projection booth, "Show that newscast from Earth, please."

The screen came on, and there stood a man with a microphone in his hand.

"This is Sam Samison reporting live from Brooklyn. Behind me lies the body of Nicky 'Knick Knack' Vocci. The fifty-six-year-old mobster was shot to death around ten this morning. Two men in a white van pulled up to the gangster's car, and one jumped out with a shotgun and opened fire. Police have caught the men but are withholding their names. In a bizarre twist given Vocci's reputation, a woman who was walking her one-year-old daughter in a stroller when the drama unfolded claims Vocci jumped in front of her and her baby to shield them from the bullets. So the question is, did Nicky Vocci die a hero? Given his history, this reporter finds it hard to believe."

The image went blank.

"To hell with him," said Nicky.

"You are charming. Well, did you?" asked Faith.

"Did I what?"

"Jump in front of the woman and her baby to save them."

"I don't know."

"Oh, that's nice."

"What is going on?"

"My job is to put souls into humans entering the world and to collect the souls that are leaving. I went to Earth today for Yolinda Perez, and instead I got you. You were supposed to live, and she was supposed to die. But you jumped in the way and saved her. Why?"

"Why not?"

"'Cause you're a fool; that's why. You were supposed to die at the age of eighty-five and become one of the Prides. However, you saved that woman's life, and now we don't know what to do. So we're going to try something."

"Try what?"

"Have you saved your soul by saving others?"

"Wait a minute, you mean I could have lived?"

"I told you that you were a simpleton."

"Okay, that's enough. Now, how am I supposed to do this?" Truth flew off the stage and pulled a sheet off of a body lying nearby. "You're going back in this," she said. "This was your and Lisa's son—or, rather, what your son would have been had you not killed Lisa."

"Lisa was pregnant?" he asked incredulously.

"Three weeks, Dummy."

"You're right, I am a dummy."

"Oh, come now. I was just kidding. The fact is, you didn't know better. Will you do it?" Truth asked.

"Go back? Yeah, okay," Nicky shrugged.

"Good for you," Faith responded.

"What kind of angels are you any way?"

Faith smiled. "The honest kind."

"Oh, how special."

"Listen, Nicky. You were full of pride, suspicion, anger, fear, lust, and insecurity. So what gives? Why would some soul like you give a rat's ass about someone else? The facts speak for themselves. You don't care about anyone. You never have."

"Wait a minute. Pride, fear, whatever ... that clip we watched said they were angels, too. So what's wrong with them?"

Truth stood up and walked to the edge of the stage. As she waved her hand, Nicky looked at her, and she began to speak. "When the planet you call Earth said you could all live on her, Pride and his followers left us to try to take over Earth. Love came up with rules, and Pride wouldn't follow them, so he and his followers struck out on their own. The spirit of the universe banned them from what you call heaven, and there has been a war over who gets what soul ever since."

Nicky went on stage with all the angels. They sat in a circle and talked. Although they were not as he imagined, they all had one thing in common: they were truly happy. They smiled and laughed and truly cared for each other. Nicky had never seen anything like it. They explained that there had always been thousands of angels trying to help their kindred souls on Earth. But as time had passed, humans had listened less and less, and Pride and his angels had begun claiming more and more souls. When a soul was full of pride, it didn't learn. Therefore, it couldn't move on, so it wandered the Earth. Their only pleasure was to torment the living.

So a deal was arranged. The head angels would pick out a soul for Nicky to help. If Nicky could get them back on track, his own soul would heal and grow, and Nicky could then move on. They also told Nicky this had to work, for the planet was growing tired of all the intolerance humans had for one another. She wanted them off of her. The angels had promised to fix it, and she had said she would give them the time they needed. But as of late, she had been growing impatient.

Nicky said he would do the best he could. The first angel he would work with was Faith. The first human Faith picked was Lily Flowers. Lily was on her second go-round on Earth. The first time she hadn't done so well. She died young, so she was given a second chance. She was not doing so well this time either. Insecurity was tormenting her, and it seemed likely she was going to take her own life. If she did that, she'll be lost in Pride's mad realm. On Earth, she was very well off, so if she did end her life, the humans on Earth would think there really is no happiness; one human life really could affect all the others. However, if Nicky could turn her around, she would fall in love. Then she would help her fellows. And in return, Nicky's soul could start to heal.

Nicky stood up in his new body on his new feet. He was thirty-five years old and handsome. Pride and his angels were looking for Nicky's soul so they could destroy it. So the angels were sending him back in a form that was never born. It was brilliant. Of course, he also needed a new name, so the angels chose Daniel Peter. They wished him luck as he went back to Earth with Faith to try and save a girl named Lily Flowers.

The Excalibur of Boca Raton stood on an island. It was Boca Raton's version of the Statue of Liberty. But the only huddled masses there were mowing lawns and pushing brooms. It stood in the middle of the Intracoastal Waterway and had its own ferry that went back and forth. This ivory tower looked like a giant rook from God's chess set, gleaming in the Florida sunshine.

Sitting behind an executive's desk was the concierge, busy minding everybody's business. White Carrara marble made the lobby always cool. It was a cross between Caesar's Roman palace and a mausoleum. The concierge looked up from his newspaper to find the doorman standing in front of him.

"What is it, Justin?"

"There's a superb-looking gentleman outside yelling at the sky in the driveway."

"The ferry left half an hour ago. Where did he come from?"

"I don't know. It's like he dropped from the sky."

"Well, go see what he wants."

"I'd like to tell him what I want. He's yummy."

As Justin walked down the Italian marble driveway, he thought to himself that 7:00 a.m. was too early for such nonsense. There he stood, right in front of Daniel Peter.

"May I help you, sir?"

"It's good to be alive!"

Mother of God, Justin thought. *He can't be from Brooklyn!* Justin had escaped from there when he was seventeen. Somehow he had survived all those years, all those beatings, only to find himself five years later face-to-face with a Brooklynite. A gorgeous one, but a Brooklynite nonetheless.

"I'm here to see Lily Flowers," replied Daniel.

Justin's heart stopped. Lily Flowers's father owned the Excalibur. She lived in the penthouse. The Flowerses were from New York, so wherever this thug came from, Lily Flowers wanted to see him; there was no time to waste. Justin noticed something odd about this man. First, he wasn't much older than Justin, yet he acted and sounded much older. Also, he was dressed in white khaki shorts and a flowered shirt—an outfit Justin would be proud to wear. *It's as though he were put here by circumstances not his own,* Justin thought.

A petite blond woman came toward them. "Daniel, are you ready?" Faith asked. "Wow! Look at you, all human."

"All human?" Justin asked.

From the lobby door, the concierge yelled, "Justin, Miss Flowers is waiting for them!" There was absolute panic in his voice. Lily Flowers and her family were the richest of the rich. They had enjoyed a life of influence. But today Lily was going to meet with real power. Heaven was on its way up the elevator.

In the elevator, Faith turned to the now Daniel Peter.

"How do you feel?"

42

"It's like I have a wet suit and scuba gear on. It's helping me get around, but it ain't me."

"You'll get used to it. You've been blessed."

"I know. I died when I wasn't supposed to, almost got to heaven, but instead wound up in my unborn son's body so I can go help someone I don't even know. And best of all, I'm in hot, sticky Florida. Yeah, I've been blessed. Oh man, I just thought of something—does this mean I'm the father and the son?"

"I never thought of that. Don't you love irony?"

Faith went on to explain that Daniel would be able to see the dead walking around. He would also see the angel Insecurity. When and if he did, he was to act natural, as if he were really alive and couldn't see a thing. She also said that when Lily was asleep or was not with him, he would go back. He would watch clips of his life and discuss what he saw with Truth. Also, more would be revealed about the rift between the angels and many other things.

"Any questions?" Faith asked as the elevators doors opened. "Sorry, sweetie, time's up!"

They stepped off the elevator, onto a marble platform, past two limestone columns, and down two marble steps. They found themselves standing in what appeared to be a living room. It was dark and cold.

Daniel called out, "Hello?"

With that, the lights came on. There stood Lily Flowers. Her hand trembled as she pulled it off the light switch. Lily was wearing gray sweatpants and a top that was two sizes too big. Her hair was tucked under a baseball cap. She had sunken brown eyes that told a tale of torment and pain.

"Hello, Miss Flowers. I'm Faith Good, and this is Daniel Peter."

"Listen, I got the telegram from my attorneys. Daniel is my new assistant. That must be you," she said as nodded her head in his direction

"Yes, it is," Daniel replied.

"Welcome, Daniel. Your room is in the servants' part of the house. The servants' elevator is there, too. Don't use this entrance again. Do whatever it is you do. I'm going back to bed."

She shut off the lights and was gone. Daniel and Faith stood in the dark for a few moments, and then, feeling along the wall, they made their way back to the servants' quarters. The kitchen was like those in restaurants. Copper pots hung on hooks above an island with a sandstone top and a built-in cutting board. Sunken into the counter was a small sink for rinsing pasta and vegetables. On the right side was a double-door oven, next to that was a flat top grill, and next to that a six-burner stove. Against the far wall was a stainless steel refrigerator. On the left side were mahogany cabinets filled with china and crystal. Beneath the counter were more cabinets and a built-in dishwasher.

There were two doors on each end of the kitchen. The door next to the fridge led into a washroom that had an ironing board, washer and dryer, and a slop sink. Next to the sink were mops and brooms in a mop bucket. The servants' elevator was there, too. There were no columns and no marble steps—just an old metal door. On the other side, across from the stove, was another door. Behind that door was Daniel's room.

It was a small room with no windows, a queen-size bed, and small nightstand with a blue lamp. Just past the walk-in closet was a sliding door leading to the bathroom that had a shower stall but no tub. In front of the bed was a nineteen-inch TV with cable. Faith and Daniel stood in the room.

"Home, sweet home," Daniel said.

"Well, sweetie, you've got a lot of work to do. I have to go."

"What the hell?" Daniel said with obvious irritation.

"Oh, stop." Faith rolled her eyes.

"But I don't know how to do this!"

"It's your job now, Daniel."

"Can't you like blink or wiggle your nose and poof— it's all done?"

"I'm an angel. I don't 'poof.' You have to do the work."

"Why this rotten job?"

"Welcome to the world of humility." And with that, Faith took her real form. Her big white wings stretched out, and she said, "Oh, wait. That's right. I can 'poof.'" And she vanished.

Daniel stood just inside the kitchen, on the threshold of the dining room. The huge, thick drapes hung shut in front of the windows, the room enveloped in a cave-like darkness. He pushed a button by the window covering. The drapes opened like curtains on a game show. The brilliant sunlight shot in, destroying the heavy darkness. Daniel stood, mouth open, as he looked out the sliding glass doors. There was a vast ocean, its waves crashing on the shore. He had been around the ocean for the whole of his first life, yet it was as though he were seeing it for the first time. He unlocked one of the sliding glass doors and stepped out onto the terrace. He saw the familiar scene of salt water as a warm breeze blew through his hair. He looked up so that the sun could warm his face. He stood still. He could feel his heartbeat, hear his breathing. He smiled to himself. One small tear fell from his left eye. His son would never have the chance to do this. Worst of all, that was the case because of him. *What kind of a man was I, and why can't I remember?*

A pair of elevator doors stood in Lily's living room. A white Italian sectional sat on top of a black marble floor. A huge flat-screen TV hung like a Picasso canvas on the wall. To the left of that was a multi-tiered Lalique crystal chandelier suspended over a Louis XVI dining table with a matching marble-top buffet. Off to the right was a barroom with a small oak counter made for serving refreshments. Goblets hung upside down on a gold rack above. Heineken was on tap, next to Ketel One vodka and other assorted expensive liquors. There were no chairs, just four round glass tables sitting on pillars at chest level. A terrace was visible just outside a sliding glass door.

The terrace wrapped completely around the outside of the penthouse which itself was a giant loop. Lily passed from the living room to the bedroom, her feet falling onto an especially plush wall-to-wall Edward Fields carpet. The room was open with blank white walls. From the antique sleigh bed, there was an excellent view of the ocean through the sliding doors.

Lily pushed a button on a remote. A section of the wall opened into a walk-in closet with custom shelves and a carousel clothes rack. When you're rich, your wardrobe has its own room. The attached bathroom had a hot tub, shower stall, and large vanity -- all white marble. In a smaller adjacent room was the toilet. Through another door was a gym, complete with all types of flex machines, a Pilates reformer, and a ballet bar in front of a mirrored wall.

On the terrace was a built-in infinity pool with a Jacuzzi, and along the edge were two tables with umbrellas and four lounge chairs.

Back inside, there was a small bedroom by a small corridor. It had a king-size bed that could be separated into two twin beds if needed. The room also had a hidden closet and a small bathroom. Down the hall was an exquisite carved-wood library with an executive desk and a pullout couch. The library connected back to the living room.

Lily Flowers sat up in bed, her heart pounding. She surveyed the room, and then she felt the nausea. With her head spinning, she felt between her legs. She hadn't met anybody the previous night. Then she experienced the horror of small memories—flashes of a night gone blank.

"Whoa!" she shouted.

There was a knock on her door. *Who would that be?* It took a moment before she remembered she'd been given a new houseman.

"Come in." The door opened, and in stepped a Greek god of a man. *How did I miss how attractive he was before,* she thought. He stood six feet two and about 215 pounds, all muscle, and had short black hair and emerald-green eyes. Lily was stuck to the bed. She wondered how he would feel on top of her. That thought was quickly replaced with *He's the help and should be treated as such.*

When Daniel stepped into the room, Lily was sitting up in bed. The bags under her eyes made her look like a raccoon. He thought to himself, *I looked better shot to death on the street*, but he just smiled and said, "Good morning." After a very short conversation, Daniel brought her tea and toast, which she ate and promptly went back to sleep. He spent the next four hours cleaning up the penthouse—dumping ashtrays, picking up the remains of shattered Waterford crystal champagne flutes, vacuuming, and mopping. How he was supposed to save her was still a mystery to him.

Daniel finished cleaning and wanted to relax, but Lily woke up and asked him to draw her a bath. She walked into the bathroom wearing a very sheer pink robe and announced that she'd be ready to eat in forty minutes. Leaving the bathroom, Daniel headed toward the kitchen and then realized that he didn't know how to cook. He didn't even want to learn. He hated housework. He hated Lily. He found himself wondering why the hell he should care about this rich bitch. As a matter of fact, if she "wished it," he'd gladly toss her off the terrace.

Arriving in the kitchen, he found Faith waiting for him.

"Hello, Daniel."

"Hi."

"How's it going?"

"I don't know how to cook. I hate cleaning. I'm a real man, you know, not some squishy sissy."

"Well, in actuality, you're a dead man walking around in the body of somebody who never got a chance to exist."

"Gee, that makes me feel a lot better."

"Just believe that I believe."

"What does that mean?" Daniel asked but without answering, Faith vanished.

In the fridge, Daniel found a filet mignon, a blue carton of mushrooms, and some onions. He also found some carrot sticks in water. He diced the onions, lined the bottom of a sauté pan with oil and put it over a medium flame. He wet the tips of his fingers with water and then flicked them toward the pan. The oil crackled, and he put in some minced garlic. The garlic smell filled the air, making his stomach dance. Next he added the chopped onions and sliced mushrooms. As they cooked, he rolled the filet in a mixture of sea salt, garlic powder, and black pepper.

When the meat was coated, he put it on a tin plate coated in olive oil and put it in the broiler at 350 degrees. He steamed six carrot sticks in a double boiler and coated them in maple syrup. He couldn't believe it. It was as if he'd been doing this his whole life. He suddenly thought of a stupid joke: *Hey, I can do anything if I have Faith.*

On a plate, he put the cooked filet in the middle and surrounded it with the carrot sticks. He then poured the sautéed mushrooms, onions, and garlic over the meat. He put the plate in the warming oven and rang the bell, and he then waited for Lily to come and eat.

Lily's voice came over an intercom. "Bring my food to the pool."

He set a place for one with gold flatware on a tray, and then, wearing an oven mitt, he placed the plate on the tray. He walked out onto the terrace, carrying the tray and walking toward the pool. He turned the corner, and saw Lily climbing out of the pool. Her long, dark hair hung dripping down her back. She was wearing a pink bikini that clung to her body. She stood up straight, tilted her head, and shook free the excess water. Her hair swayed back and forth as droplets of water jumped to freedom and her large breasts bounced as if trying to free themselves from the cloth covering them. Daniel stood captive in the moment. His mouth went dry. As his eyes took in the beauty, his brain screamed, *Calm down!*

She turned to him, smiled, and sat down at one of the umbrella tables. Daniel trembled slightly as he placed the tray in front of her.

"Have a seat," she said, gesturing toward a chair.

He sat across from her and waited for his breath to return. She looked at him and smiled again. Her teeth were pearl-white— perfect. She had dazzling hazel eyes; the black under them was gone. It must have been mascara. She was stunning. How could he possibly resist her?

They sat and made small talk and she complimented him on the meal.

Lily had received a telegram from her father's people. He was in Europe, but he'd found someone to "help her." That person was Daniel. Lily was in trouble. A few days ago, driving her Mercedes SL500 while stoned out of her mind on A1A, she had the top down with her toy poodle, Lucky, in the car. She'd been speeding and wavering on the thin two-lane highway, and Lucky had jumped from the car to his death. She'd lost control of the car and driven through a fence onto the beach in Del Ray. She jumped out of the car and fled.

One of her friends had a summerhouse just down the road. Lily tried to hide out there; however, it was 10:00 a.m. on a Tuesday morning, so there were a lot of witnesses. The police traced her to the friend's house, but Lily refused to come out. She voluntarily surrendered herself after about a half-hour of negotiating with the police. She was charged with DWI, resisting arrest, reckless endangerment, animal cruelty, and a host of other charges. Attorneys had her released on bail within an hour of her arrest. That was last Friday. She received the telegram on Saturday, and now it was Monday and here was Daniel, just as promised—or, rather, threatened.

Daniel had just finished cleaning up the kitchen when Lily called on the intercom and requested he go downstairs to get the Bentley ready. In the washroom, there was a board with hooks and keys hanging from it. He took the keys marked "Bentley." The elevator stopped at the parking garage. He found Lily's car; the front license plate read "Pic-N-Flowers." Daniel rolled his eyes when he saw it. He pulled the white sedan up to the front of the building and waited.

Lily finally came down the driveway. She had her hair in a ponytail and it bobbed as she walked. Her long, tan legs looked perfect in her white sailing shorts. She was a vision of beauty, a pleasure for any eye to behold. Daniel was perplexed as to how such beauty could hide such ugliness. Lily jumped into the backseat, and Daniel drove the car onto the ferry.

Lily told Daniel to drive to Palm Beach. They were going to Brook Stein's residence. Daniel thought, *Wow, Brook Stein! Who the hell is Brook Stein?* Daniel got on I-95 at Palmetto Park which was, as always, chaotic. The drivers were all choreographers of peril. Daniel had both hands on the wheel, checking his mirrors every ten seconds. He was going eighty miles an hour, and cars were flying past as if he were parked.

"I hate Florida!" he yelled.

Lily laughed in the backseat as she took a flask from her purse and drank. Then she pulled out a small vial. She dug some white powder out with a tiny spoon and snorted it. She did the same using her other nostril. Her eyes teared up, and she gagged. She sniffed harder and took another drink. She then smiled and fell back into the seat.

Richard Stein was an attorney for the wealthy. His daughter, Brook, was Lily Flowers's best friend. The two girls had done it all together, and today Brook and her boyfriend of the month, Cal, were hosting a yacht party. Cal was just like Brook— late twenties, good-looking, spoiled, selfish, and lazy—as were most of the attendees.

Daniel and Lily pulled up to Richard Stein's mansion in the Bentley. A valet greeted the car and opened Lily's door. Lily walked around to the driver's side of the car. Daniel put his window down, and Lily handed him a black AMEX card. She told him to go to the cleaners and pick up her clothes. He was also to go to the liquor store in the shopping center, where Lily had already called in her order. She told Daniel the card was his to use to get whatever supplies they needed, and every Friday he was to bring the receipts to the family accountant. The accountant would give him his pay.

"But we'll go over all that tonight; just get my clothes and liquor. Any questions?"

"Do you want the clothes and liquor, or liquor and clothes?"

Lily smiled and walked away as Daniel watched her. *You've got a great future behind you,* he thought. He put the Bentley in drive and pulled away.

Looking in his rearview mirror, he saw all sorts of limos and even a Hummer pulling in behind him. He pulled out of the driveway and headed south on A1A. This was more his style—a two-lane road, thirty miles per hour, and an ocean view. He drove along, listening to Dean Martin's "Everybody Love Somebody" when Faith appeared in the backseat. He was startled and lost control of the car. He was headed for a huge palm tree, and then wham! He was back on the road, safe and sound.

"You should really be more careful when driving," Faith said.

"Me? You pop in and out of thin air and scare the crap out of me, and I should be more careful?"

"Yes, you should."

"You could've killed us!"

"I'm an angel, and you're dead. Where's the probability? Besides, you're back on the road now, safe and sound. It's time for your first lesson with Truth."

"I'm not going anywhere until you answer me. How does that grab you?" And with that, Daniel disappeared.

Daniel was back in the auditorium. The big exit doors swung open, and in walked Truth, her long, silky brown hair parted in the middle. She wore a lacy nightgown. He could just make out the characteristics of her womanly form. She had a delicate face, and protruding from her shoulder blades were white wings. There was something special about this deity; she was beaming with integrity. Daniel realized that was something he had never known. She sat down next to him and spoke.

"Today we are going to watch your last day on Earth. But before we do, I will fill you in on the events that led to your demise."

Truth told Daniel about a mobster named Ray Curry who was a soldier in the Chips crew. He lived in Marine Park on 34th and Fillmore and had a nice house with his wife, Carole, his son, Jim, who was twelve, and his ten-year-old daughter, Kelly. Everyone suspected what Ray did for a living —everyone but his family. Or so it seemed. It didn't matter; people wouldn't say what they thought of Ray out loud. He was just another middle-class working guy. Ray was Irish Italian, which meant he could work for the family but could never become a made man. Chips paid him well, and he was a hit man in good standing, so he didn't care. He thought Carole had a boyfriend. Nicky insisted he was paranoid. Chips and the Hump also agreed. That was because Nicky was her boyfriend. He told Chips and the Hump that Ray wasn't doing the right thing. Carole was lonely and a great lay, so he wasn't going to stop banging her.

Truth ended the story, the lights were dimmed, and the projector turned on.

A mental impression came from the screen. There was Nicky getting dressed. Carole lay naked on the bed.

"You really know how to make a woman happy," she purred.

Nicky finished getting dressed. On his way out of the bedroom, he turned toward her.

"It amazes me how you can screw me in your husband's bed."

"That's because all he wants to do is sleep in the bed."

"That's because you're the mother of his children. He doesn't know you're a slut."

He turned and walked out of the bedroom.

"You'll be back for more, you prick!" Carole yelled from the bedroom as Nicky walked down the stairs and turned right at the bottom of the flight. He was smiling as he walked through the dining room and kitchen and down some steps to a side door leading to the driveway. As Nicky approached his car, Ray Curry suddenly jumped out of the shadows. He had a surprised look on his face.

"Nicky? What the hell are you doing at my house at two a.m.?"

"Oh, come on, Ray, I was just finishing your wife again." Nicky jumped back, pulled his 9 mm from his holster, and shot Ray right between the eyes. With one shot, Ray was dead. Nicky stood in the driveway for about fifteen minutes, not moving, listening for sirens. Marine Park and 34th Street were quiet. He grinned and walked back into the house, where Carole stood at the top of the stairs.

"What the hell did you do?" she yelled.

Nicky walked up the stairs with his arms open. He told her not to scream and said that he had done it so they could be together. He told her how much he loved her. When he reached the top of the stairs, she collapsed into his arms. He held her as she sobbed heavily on his shoulder. He moved around, and when the position was right, he threw her down the stairs, breaking her neck. He stepped over the body and called Chips and the Hump to help him clean up. He knew the neighbors would figure it was those crazy mobsters. No one was gonna say anything.

By 7:00 a.m., it looked like the Curry family had gone out for the day.

Jim Curry was Ray's older brother. He knew what Ray did for a living and which family he was affiliated with. He didn't care. Knick Knack, Chips, and the Hump were as good as dead. He was gonna get his revenge, and he'd kill any Guinea mobster that got in his way.

The morning after the murders, Avenue U was empty. It was Sunday morning, and most people were asleep or at Sunday mass. As Nicky drove down to the bakery at 13th Street, he passed a young mother on the sidewalk, pushing her baby in a carriage. Nicky thought to himself, *with a body like that, she'd have twelve kids if she were my wife.* He laughed under his breath and parked his car behind a white van. As he got out of the car, the van doors burst open. Jim Curry jumped out with a shotgun, slipped on the pavement, and landed on his behind. Nicky laughed out loud and reached for his own gun. Out of the corner of his eye, he spotted the young mother with the carriage. Nicky jumped across the hood of his car.

"Look out!" he yelled. Jim scrambled to his feet. Nicky stood in front of the young mother, and Curry shot him twice in the chest. Nicky fell to the sidewalk, dead.

The lights came up, and the projector spun to a stop. Daniel sat with his, mouth open, confused.

56

"Why, after fifty-six years of doing whatever you wanted to whomever you wanted, would you give your life for a stranger?" Truth asked. "You didn't have to. I'm sorry, but I don't get it."

Daniel shrugged his shoulders, and the two sat in silence. Truth waited for Daniel to take it all in. After a few minutes, an image appeared on the screen. It was another angel. She had a gray business suit, and her hair was pulled back tight. She wore round glasses. She appeared intellectual, but her shapely legs gave her sex appeal. She carried a briefcase in one hand and a ledger under her arm.

"Hey, I saw her right before I got shot. I remember thinking, 'I bet she's got a body to match those legs.'"

"That's nice, but her name is Consequence. She lives on Earth with the humans and combative angels. She keeps a balance between life and death."

"Death? That sweet thing is Death? Hey, what a way to go."

"I'm guessing Lust was one of your favorite angels."

"Lust is an angel?"

"An earth angel, one of the Pride servants. Can we get this lesson down before we move on?"

"I was just sayin'."

"Shut up and pay attention. I'm just sayin'."

"I'm all yours."

Truth rolled her eyes. "Okay, everything on Earth is a direct result of its action. Consequence keeps a tally in her ledger. The briefcase is full of reports on all living things on the planet, plus reports on Mother Earth herself. She does an awesome job."

"She watches everybody on the planet?" asked Daniel puzzled.

"That's right, and humans make her job harder, because you are all born with free will."

"Free will is a bitch."

"Do you have any idea what I'm talking about?" Faith asked.

"No," Daniel admitted.

"So why don't you ask me any questions?"

"I don't know," he shrugged.

"Because you're still full of pride!"

"So what?"

"That's a good answer. Humans who choose pride never learn. I'm done with you. I'll send you to Pride's mad realm so you can wander the earth endlessly. Good luck."

"Wait!" Daniel said reluctantly. "I'll do whatever it takes. Give me a chance, please!"

"Okay, one more chance. You'd better pay attention."

"Okay, okay. Wow, I had no idea angels were so mean."

Faith stood with her hands on her hips and asked, "Are you finished?"

"Yeah."

"You were never supposed to be here. However, you took action, and that action changed your consequence, understand?"

"Could you go a little slower?" Daniel requested.

"Let's talk about the human soul."

Truth explained, "The soul is a piece of the spirit of the universe. It's like an infant child placed into a coat of bones and skin. This coat, however, doesn't last. It wasn't made to. The soul never dies. It is reborn again and again, and like an infant child, the soul learns and grows. Angels were created to guide, help, and raise these infant souls. Pride wanted these human souls for himself. He wanted to be loved and worshipped. He convinced Fear, Anger, Lust, Insecurity, and Suspicion to join him. They have been leading souls astray ever since."

"So, like, it's not my fault? I'm an innocent? It's the prick Pride's fault?"

"Not exactly, Daniel."

"You just said Pride and yada yada—you know, his crew— they're the ones you guys want? I'm just a victim?"

"Oh, shut up!" Truth said, losing her patience.

"Oh, nice move, angel! 'Shut up?' You said 'Shut up' to me? You're supposed to be nice. Now again, if I'm being led astray, how is that my fault?"

"Watch your temper, Daniel."

"Or what? You're gonna kill me?"

Truth took a deep breath. She wasn't going to enrage him. She knew that whenever one is angry, one is wrong, and Daniel was still full of the combative angels. She felt it was better to ignore him and go on with the lesson.

"Free will," she said.

"Free what?"

"Along with the soul, humans were given a brain. This instrument of intelligence records experience. One can gain this only from having lived. Free will is the propulsion that makes the mind work. No other organism has been given this gift. Humans must learn the proper use of free will."

"And how do I do that?"

"To love others as you love yourself."

"Get the —— outta here with that cliché!"

"You were given a second chance because you gave that woman your life," countered the angel.

"Oh, so I can be a real pain in the ass. I just gotta save some bitch and it's like I'm not wicked at all."

"Do you know what 'wicked' means, Daniel?"

"You're gonna tell me, aren't you?"

"Wickedness is belief in pride. When you think wrongly and build up false conditions, you suffer the consequences. When you were Nicky, you were—and still are—full of the combative angels. Or, as humans say, you were evil."

"So how does an evil guy like me ever make it into heaven? Oh, wait a second, by saving that rotten spoiled brat, right?"

"Yes, Daniel. Save Lily Flowers."

"I'd rather go back and toss her off the balcony."

"Daniel, if you can't help Lilly, you're doomed to go to Pride's mad realm. You'll wander the earth forever. Lost. With no peace or happiness."

Daniel sighed.

"How can I possibly help her? I killed the mother of my child. I've killed at least thirty people…and now you want me to save someone? To help God? Are you nuts?"

"You can do it. Find the love in your soul. It *is* there," Truth responded calmly.

"The love in my soul? What love? Listen, Bambi, I ain't ever been loved, nor do I need to be. Maybe we should just forget this whole thing. If I'm supposed to be with Pride, so be it. I'll deal. Hell, I'll kick Pride's ass and take over."

Behind them, the exit doors opened, and in walked Faith. She wore a blissful smile on her face and came at them, almost skipping.

"Hey, Daniel, ready to go back and get to work?"

"I was just telling Truth I don't wanna do this."

"Let me say this so you'll understand. Who gives a damn what you want? You're gonna save Lily Flowers because that's what we want," said Faith forcefully.

Daniel sighed again. "Whatever."

"Good! Now get up; let's go!"

"You're my kind of angel. Besides, I can't take any more information."

"Truth tends to think too much. She always needs to find the answers."

"Hello?" said Truth. "I'm still here. Can you two act like it?"

"Aw, sweetie, I love ya; you know that," Faith replied.

"You know, Faith, if it's so easy to teach them, why don't you do it?"

"Truth, no one said it was easy, but why don't you talk his language?"

"Just... just take him away. I'll see him later. This lesson is officially over."

"I know this is gonna work, Truth," said the other angel.

"You always 'know it's gonna work', Faith."

"And I'm always right."

Truth shrugged. "I hope so."

Daniel interjected, "Yo, so let's do this! You're killing me here."

"You're already dead," Faith and Truth said together.

❖

Daniel opened his eyes in Lily's penthouse. He was in his room, on the bed when the phone rang.

"Hello?"

"Hey, babycakes, I'm ready to come home," Lily slurred. *Great. She's drunk out of her mind*, he thought. Daniel went downstairs, got the Bentley, and headed back for Palm Beach. As he drove, Faith appeared in the backseat. Daniel was no longer surprised.

"There's one weapon humans have that Pride and his angels have no power over."

"And what would that be?"

"Laughter. Life is to be enjoyed." With that, Faith disappeared.

Daniel drove on and looked in the rearview mirror. *Who am I supposed to be, Jerry Lewis? Let the healing begin. Har har har.*

TO SAVE A SOUL: PART 2

aniel drove the Bentley up the marble driveway. He pulled behind another Bentley. A handsome chauffeur appeared, and in broken English asked, "Here for Miss Flowers, no?"

"That's right. Daniel Peter for Miss Flowers." Daniel stuck out his hand to shake. The Latino chauffeur looked at his hand and turned away.

"Sorry, me no like touch."

"Whatever. Where is she?"

The chauffeur led him to a golf cart. Both men got in and began to drive around the grounds.

"Miss Flowers at pool house," the driver said as they pulled up to two huge gates. "We here; she there."

Daniel climbed out, and the chauffeur waved and drove off.

"Thanks a lot, pal!" Daniel yelled. He turned, walked through the gates, and saw the pool house. It looked like a miniature White House. The pool was heart-shaped. Daniel wondered if Julius Caesar used to live there. He saw Lily and a young man standing together on the other side of the pool. She waved, and Daniel walked toward them. As he got closer, the young man moved behind Lily and reached around to grabbed her breasts.

"Stop it!" Lily shouted.

Daniel walked faster, holding his hand up. "Easy, pal!"

The young man stepped in front of Lily. He was brawny but elegant looking. "Who the —— do you think you're talking to?" he sneered at Daniel.

Lily grabbed his arm. "Stop, Heath. He's my houseman."

"Teach him his place!" Heath said, shaking Lily's hand off.

Daniel walked right up to Heath, almost chest to chest. Heath stared at him, his hands clenched in fists. Out of the corner of his eye, Daniel saw three other young men coming out of the huge trees and bushes that surrounded the pool. It was like a mock version of the Garden of Eden. He looked toward Lily. She was frozen with her mouth open. He wondered why she had this look of utter astonishment on her face. Then came a hard shove that sent him back. Heath walked right at Daniel and shoved him harder.

The other three young men started shouting,"That's it, Heath; get that guy!"

Heath went to shove Daniel again, and Daniel twisted, grabbed Heath under his arm, and flipped him over. Heath hit the concrete pavement surrounding the pool—hard. He landed hip first. The impact took his breath away and he lay there helpless.

Standing over him, Daniel whispered, "You're done, fool." Daniel glared at the other three. They stood there silent, in shock.

"Come on; you want me? I'm here; let's go!"

Lily grabbed Daniel. "Please take me home!"

They had a long walk back to the car. Lily was completely silent as Daniel drove them back to Boca Raton. Lily opened the minibar and began to drink heavily. Still she said nothing. When they got back, Daniel had to carry her in because she had passed out in the backseat. He laid her on her bed and made sure she was on her stomach in case she got sick. Then Daniel went to his room, lay down on his back on the bed, and turned on the TV.

The sun moved secretly behind the ocean. The night sky began to withdraw. In this endeavor, crimson was the color of the morning. As the sky turned blue, puffy clouds of white came to enhance the inception of the new day. Daniel was standing on the terrace, watching the sunrise, when he heard lily come up behind him. She was wearing a gray sweatsuit and baseball cap.

"You all right, kid?" Daniel asked.

"Thank you for saving me."

"Who was that moron?"

"Heath Stein, Brook's brother."

"Heath? What happened? Mom and Dad wanted a cat?"

Lily started to giggle. "I guess so."

Lily told Daniel and she and Heath were buddies—no love, no relationship, just sex. Although she liked the way he looked and felt, she couldn't stand him as a person. She kept trying to break it off, but they were always invited to the same places and would always party together, and the next thing they knew, bang, they'd be doing it. The day before at the pool, he'd been begging her for sex, but Lily had told herself that this time she was determined to not give in. As he talked, he flirted and flattered her. She noticed he kept looking toward the bushes. After a while, she couldn't resist his charm any longer and gave in. She agreed to go down on him, but that was it. Lily gave him pleasure and had to admit she enjoyed it as always. They had just finished when Daniel showed up, and when Heath's friends ran out of the bushes, she realized why he had been so insistent. Heath had wanted them to watch, and Lily had inadvertently given them quite a show. Lily was far from being a prude, but putting on a sex show for the amusement of Heath and his buddies was not something she would ever knowingly choose to do. She began sobbing.

Daniel took her in his arms so Lily could cry on his shoulder. It was then that Daniel felt it: a strange feeling—something he'd never felt before.

Compassion.

It flowed through him and filled him with warmth. There's a funny thing about kindness and compassion. The more you give, the better you feel. As he held Lily, the sensation of feeling lighter coursed through him, as if he were carrying heavy luggage up endless flights of stairs and most of the bags were falling off.

Lily stopped sobbing, and Daniel said, "Hey, let's go for a walk on the beach."

As the pair walked along the beach, the waves crashed along the shore. In the background was the pier. Along this stretch of A1A, the hotels touched the sky, their shaded glass gleaming in the sunshine. Tiki bars served drinks with umbrellas and the palm trees formed a chorus line and danced in the breeze. It looked like a living postcard.

Lily began collecting seashells. The breeze played with her hair. She'd trot over to a spot and move the sand with her feet. "Oh my God!" She'd say with exuberance. Then she'd bend over and scoop up her prize from the sand. She'd hold the shell in her palm, bring it up to her lips, and blow off the excess sand. She looked as innocent as a child.

Before they'd left for the beach, Lily had showered and changed. Daniel thought it odd to shower to go to the beach. Lily was wearing her little white shorts and a pink tank top. She put on a silk shirt covered with flowers over the tank top. Her hair was parted in the middle, with white barrettes on each side to keep the hair out of her eyes. With her twinkling eyes and dimples, she looked like the all-American dream girl. Daniel couldn't contain the love building in his heart. He wished that these moments would last forever.

The two walked side by side along the shore. Lily told Daniel how much better she felt. Then she stopped, looked into his eyes, and asked, "Can I call you Dannyboy? I love guys with nicknames that end in 'boy,' like Tommyboy or Johnnyboy."

Daniel staggered backward. "Lisa, is that you?" His face went pale and tears welled up in his eyes.

Lily looked at him nervously. "Who's Lisa? What's wrong with you?"

Daniel quickly shifted gears and collected himself. "Sorry, I'm okay. You just reminded me of somebody I knew."

"You're nuts!" Lily said, laughing off the incident. Then she smiled gently and asked, "Did you love this Lisa very much?"

"Very, very much."

"So you two broke up?"

"She died."

"Oh my God, I'm so sorry. Was it recently?"

"A lifetime ago."

"How old was she?" Lily asked softly.

"Young. I don't remember."

"How did she die? Was it cancer? A car wreck?"

"What the difference does it make?" Daniel's voice rose. "She died. End of story." Daniel looked at Lily who took a step back. "Lily, I'm really sorry; I didn't mean that."

"You really loved her. I understand it must be hard to lose somebody like that. I was being nosy. She's gone; that's all that matters."

"She used to forgive my temper too. You remind me a lot of her. Beautiful, kind, smart."

"I don't know about all that. I do a lot of stupid things."

"You're young; you're supposed to. Everyone does dumb things when they're young. How else can you learn?"

"Did Lisa love you back?"

"Yeah, she did. You know, it's funny. A lot of people were scared of me—you know, with my temper and all. But not Lisa. She wouldn't put up with my nonsense. I used to love her for that. She had me, and she knew it."

"It must be wonderful to be loved like that," Lily said with tears in her eyes. Lily told Daniel that when she was a baby, her mother started running around on her father. Her mother was a runway model when she met Lily's father in Paris. After a whirlwind romance, she quit modeling, and they got married.

Five years later, she had Lily. It turned out motherhood wasn't her thing, so for a boatload of cash and a house in the south of France, she divorced Lily's father and left him to raise Lily by himself. Lily was eighteen months old, and her mother left her for a better lifestyle. Lily's childhood was one of boarding schools and nannies. The only love she got came from strangers. She had money, power—everything except what she really wanted: parents, a family, and a place to belong.

Daniel could barely breathe as sorrow and conflict ravaged his soul. If this was really Lisa, would they still be together? Would she be happy? Would they be married, and how many kids would they have? What if he hadn't killed her? What would have happened? If it was not Lisa, then why was he thinking like this? He shook off those thoughts, and the two of them walked back to the private ferry that took them home.

When they got home, Daniel made tuna fish sandwiches for lunch. As they sat and ate on the terrace, the phone rang and Daniel took the call. The front desk said there was a Heath Stein to see Miss Flowers. Daniel told them he'd go down and take Mr. Stein up himself. The elevator door opened and in stepped Heath Stein. He wore a gray suit, and his hair was perfectly coiffed. In his hand were two dozen perfect long-stemmed white roses. The elevator doors closed, and the ascent to the penthouse began.

Daniel grabbed the roses from Heath and began to beat him on the head. He grabbed Heath by the throat and said in an ominous voice, "There's a new sheriff in town, and the law is this: Lily gets hurt no more. Get it, pumpkin? Now get along, little dogie, and don't come back, or off the terrace you go. Now beat it."

The doors opened and Daniel stepped out. Heath remained in the corner of the elevator. The doors closed, and the elevator descended. As Daniel crossed through the living room on the way to the kitchen, Lily came out.

"Where's Heath?"

"You won't see him no more."

"What the does that mean?"

Lily kept yelling that Daniel was her employee, a servant. She yelled that he should stick to his job description or else, saying that Heath's father and her father were best friends, that she and Heath had grown up together, that Heath's sister, Brook, was her best friend, and on and on and on.

She stormed off, and he heard her make a phone call. When she came back in the room, she was dressed to kill in the tightest black sheath he'd ever seen. She ordered Daniel to clean the penthouse and said she'd be back with Heath that night. Daniel was to make an elaborate dinner and have several bottles of wine chilled correctly. Finally she stepped into the elevator, the doors closed, and it began its descent. Daniel stood there, confused. Faith appeared.

"Good job, kiddo! Nicky, lose your temper; that will help."

"You know what? I want to wander the earth. I want to serve Pride. 'Help someone, Daniel, yeah! Then you'll be an angel!' I must've been mad. Let me go for the last time. Let me go to hell."

"There's no such place as hell," Faith retorted.

"Well, wherever the place is you send people like me."

"All right, Daniel, let's stop now. Control yourself."

"Tell me this Lily what's-her-face isn't my Lisa."

"At the time you knew her, she was Lisa. But you killed her, and at that moment, she became Lily. Her soul was brand-new, so it was sent right back. But Lisa is dead; she had her lifetime. She took actions that put her in a position to be killed. Now this soul is again taking negative actions, only this time she'll wind up with Pride. Now, control your emotional nature."

"My what?"

"Anger and violence never end well. When you make a decision based on emotion, you're always wrong. Please, sweetie, try to understand."

"Let me get this straight. I'm in my son's body—my son who was never born. I'm here to protect the woman I killed who was carrying my son when I killed them both. And you want me not to get emotional?"

"It won't help, Daniel."

"What happened to my son's soul?"

"It was moved too, but don't worry about that. This could just confuse you."

"Confuse me? Yeah, to say the least. Holy crap, if I'm in my son's body, then I'm father and son."

"Shakespeare's got nothing on us."

"Oh, that's so funny I forgot to laugh."

"Listen up. You're not the father or the son. She is Lily Flowers, and you're Daniel Peter. Nicky and Lisa are gone. Their lives have ended; that's it. This is now, and you're here to save your soul by saving Lily's. Forget about your son; he was never born."

"So… what am I supposed to do?"

"Clean the house, make dinner, and go from there."

"Thanks for all your help."

"Anytime, sweetie. Good-bye for now." And with that, Faith disappeared.

Daniel cleaned the penthouse with intensity, fighting off emotions of anger. When he was finished, the suite was immaculate. The delivery boy from Monarch Prime Cuts came with Lily's meat order. There was enough chicken, steak, and veal for a month. Daniel decided to make veal parmesan, angel hair pasta, and garlic bread.

As the marinara sauce simmered, he set out three bowls. He put flour in the first, egg in the second, and breadcrumbs in the third. He'd just begun to dip the veal in the flour when he heard Lily and Heath laughing as the elevator doors open. Daniel came out of the kitchen to find the couple leaning against the elevator door, talking in conspiratorial whispers. Lily could barely stand up.

As Daniel approached, Lily slurred, "Dannall, Danyell, apologize to Mr. Stein."

Daniel was taken aback for a moment. He sucked in some air and then stated flatly, "I'm very sorry, Mr. Stein."

"As well you should be! I don't comprehend just who you think you are!" Heath sneered.

"I do hope you can accept my apology. I have no excuse for my behavior," Daniel responded in monotone.

Heath escalated his sneering tone. "Nothing wrong with your behavior; you're low-life scum, and you behave accordingly."

"Heath, stop it! Daniel, you may leave us now," Lily commanded.

Daniel turned on his heel and walked back into the kitchen. He then stopped and looked back. Heath was squeezing Lily's ass. Heath noticed Daniel watching, stuck out his tongue, and held up his middle finger.

Daniel continued into the kitchen, his heart pounding. He sat on the floor and banged his head against the refrigerator. He rocked back and forth, anger burning hot in his soul. He was so mad his eyes were tearing. He wanted to kill the both of them, but he knew he couldn't kill them both. He'd just kill Heath. No, he couldn't kill Heath; that was his old life. He was supposed to be here to help. He had to help Lily. He sat there and continued rocking.

"No, no, no, no, no," he repeated to himself. But no matter how hard he tried, he couldn't suppress the anger.

Then Daniel exploded.

He stood up and took a carving knife out of the drawer. Now he was blinded by rage. It was not his fault; they needed to be taught a lesson. Daniel slithered silently out of the kitchen. He could hear Lily and Heath in the cocktail alcove. An ambush was one of his fortes.

Then, above the buzzing of drunken banter, Daniel heard, "You stupid bitch!" He dropped the knife instinctively and ran into the alcove. Lily lay flat on the floor, holding her right eye. Heath was standing over her.

Daniel grabbed Health and pushed him to the edge of the terrace. Heath's face turned ashen white, and his eyes opened wide. Before he knew it, Daniel had Heath's arm twisted behind his back. He bent Heath over almost to his waist by applying his arm to Heath's head and neck. Daniel shoved Heath toward the terrace. The glass doors were open; otherwise, Heath's head would have become a battering ram. As Heath was forced onto the terrace and shoved closer toward the outside wall, he realized this madman was really going to toss him to his death. He began to plead and cry. He even urinated himself.

Daniel had this wise-ass exactly where he wanted him. As he neared the wall, he intended to push him over headfirst. But then compassion came upon him, and for the first time ever, someone else's pain bothered him. He tried to disregard these feelings, but they were stronger than anger. Daniel stopped suddenly. Heath's head swayed over the ledge of the outer wall. Then something clicked in Daniel's head.

He let go of Heath and threw him onto the floor. Heath hit the ground, crying, "Thank you, oh God, thank you!"

As Heath lay on the floor of the terrace whimpering, Daniel wanted to kick him hard, but he couldn't. Instead he picked him up by the shirt collar, dragged him to the elevator, and tossed him inside. Heath slammed face-first into the back of the elevator, moaning and crying as the elevator automatically descended.

Daniel went back into the alcove. He stood over Lily. Her eye was bright red and swollen shut, and her nose was leaking blood. In a rush of words, Lily told Daniel that Heath had come with a gram of cocaine that he had laid out on the mirror. She'd accidentally knocked her drink over all the coke. That's why Heath had hit her this time. He'd hit her before, and she didn't know why she'd kept going back to him, but she saw now that it was finally over. Finally, she saw that Heath was just another person who had pretended to care about her.

Daniel picked Lily up off the floor. He carried her into her bedroom and laid her gently on the bed.

"Daniel, I'm so sorry. I'm so messed up. I don't know who to trust. I'll never turn my back on you again," Lily said with conviction.

"Yeah, until the next time."

"There won't be a next time, I swear!" Lily implored.

"Just go to sleep, Lily."

"Please don't leave me!" she pleaded.

Much to his surprise, Daniel felt sorry for Lily. Maybe she couldn't help being the way she was. After all, Daniel had been given a second chance, so who was he to judge? He walked over and sat on the bed, gently touching Lily's face with his hands.

"What am I gonna do with you?"

"Be my friend?" Lily asked.

"If you want a friend, you gotta be a friend."

"What the hell does that mean?"

"I don't know. I can't believe I just said that." Daniel laughed.

Lily sat up on the bed and laughed too, and once again she jumped into Daniel's arms. After they embraced, Lily let herself fall back against the propped-up pillows. Daniel stayed perched at the edge of the bed. The two of them talked for hours.

Lily told Daniel that she'd really never felt at home anywhere or with anyone. The penthouse was really a summerhouse. Her father had given it to her so she wouldn't bother him or his girlfriend. Lily had felt pushed aside her whole life. And now, when she might be going to jail, her father wouldn't even come help her in person. Instead he had sent yet another attorney. For that matter, he'd sent Daniel, too. So at first she'd found it hard to believe that Daniel really cared about her, thinking that his actions were just part of his job description.

Daniel told her that her father hadn't exactly sent him but that he'd wanted to come. He said that he, too, felt like an outcast, and didn't know whom to trust. He also told her that at one time, he'd done some very bad things, but now he might be able to do something good. And he really, genuinely wanted to help Lily. But before anything could begin, before any friendship could develop, there had to be honesty and trust. The two held hands, and then Lily pointed to a row of children's books in the bookcase in corner.

"I have all these beautiful children's books. I've had them since I was a little girl. My dad bought them for me. They're special editions of Grimm's Fairy Tales with beautiful illustrations. He bought them for me, but never once did he read me even one of the stories."

At that, Daniel stood up and got a chair. He walked over to the bookcase and selected one of the volumes. He sat the chair down by the side of the bed.

Lily grabbed the book from his hands and flipped through the pages. "This one please," she whispered.

Daniel sat down and began to read "The Twelve Dancing Princesses" to Lily.

Right before Lily fell asleep, she murmured, "I knew you really wouldn't have thrown Heath off the terrace, Daniel. You're too sweet." Daniel just smiled, leaned over, and kissed the sleeping Lily on her forehead, and then he went out to straighten up the apartment.

Faith opened the auditorium doors to find Truth sitting in there, just staring.

"Honey, are you all right? Why are you still in the flesh?" Faith asked.

"I found it quite comfortable. It's soft. It's very light and wears nice. Moves and stretches."

"It's tissue."

"I love the whole suit. The mirror, lens for viewing, the hearing devices for recording."

"Stop. What's wrong? Come on; tell me."

"Faith, I had a talk with Mother Earth, and she's not happy."

"Oh please, she's never been the same since that flooding thing failed."

"It failed because of your warning that it was coming."

"Can we let the past go, Truth?"

"You're right. I'm sorry. Anyhow, she knows that Daniel was about to kill again."

"No, he wasn't," Faith reminded her. "He thought about it, but he didn't do it."

"Earth wants to know why, out of all the human souls, we would pick a psycho killer and a drunken slut to save humankind."

"I hope you told her it's because there's good in everyone. All they need is someone to help them find it."

"I don't want Earth to destroy humankind. I don't want any more souls lost to Pride. But we're depending on a completely bewitched soul to help a completely lost soul. How is it going to work?" Truth looked baffled.

"Because they have love in their souls. You'll see; they'll find it together and heal each other."

"Well, you're right. Love can do anything. I just hope this works before Mother Earth gets fed up."

"Oh, stop worrying. Now take off that skin, and let's go dancing and laughing."

"Dancing and laughing—my favorites! Let's go."

TO SAVE A SOUL: PART 3

Three months passed. During this time, Lily and Daniel grew very close. Lily had even stopped partying. The two would go to the beach or go shopping at night or watch movies. Daniel had become a great cook.

Today, Daniel dropped Lily off at Judge Amy Roth's chambers. The Flowers' family attorney had negotiated a deal. Lily walked into Judge's chambers to find Liam Patrick and her lawyer sitting next to each other. Lily couldn't stand Liam. To Lily and her friends, he was known as Saint Crazy. At six-feet-five inches tall, 230 pounds, and with strawberry-blond hair and blue eyes, to say he looked Irish would be like saying the Pope looked Catholic. Liam was only thirty-three years old; however, in his short life he'd helped countless people. Liam had a good soul. Actually, he was an old soul that had been back several times. This soul was on its last visit to Earth. After this time, he'd graduate and move on.

When Liam was seventeen, he went to college at Notre Dame. While there in his freshman year, he tried out for the football team and, as a walk-on, made third-string quarterback. That season Notre Dame started 0–4. More importantly, both the first-string and second-string quarterbacks got injured, so the coach threw Liam in. The team won for the rest of the season and Liam set a freshman completion and touchdown record. Of course, he was offered a scholarship. Liam did not want or need this. His family was very wealthy, and he went out for the football team just to see if he could make it. He turned down the football scholarship in the hopes that somebody who needed it would get it.

The Patrick family was also very powerful. Liam's great-grandfather, Kerry Patrick, was a poor Irish carpenter. He came to America in 1822 and settled in Brooklyn at the age of fourteen. Ten years later, he was building custom furniture for New York's richest families. From that one store came a chain of ten stores named Patrick's Custom Handcrafted Furniture.

Although generation after generation the family became more diversified in their careers, they still made handcrafted furniture. The values of family and honest hard work were also passed on. Liam, was an only child like Lily, and the last descendant of Kerry Patrick.

Liam graduated Notre Dame with two masters' degrees: one in engineering and the other in business administration. He went out into the world and started building homeless shelters. He started training programs for the poor at high schools so they could enter the workforce at decent pay rates. He helped hospitals build wings for children with terminal illnesses. He also helped the elderly with their medication and home services. Liam believed he could be the change that made the world better.

About nine years ago, Liam had met Judge Roth while on vacation in Hawaii. He was twenty-two, she, forty-four and a newly elected judge. The two spent three weeks together.

Now Liam was that cat-that-ate-the-canary smile that Judge Roth wore on her face sometimes, and she was the musing stare Liam sometimes went into.

Now that Lily's father had donated a million dollars to PETA, Lily went to therapy once a week. There was only one thing left to do: release Lily Flowers into the care of Liam Patrick for one year. If, during that time, she failed to comply with Liam and the duties he assigned her, the deal would be off the table and she would go to trial and, more than likely, to jail.

Judge Roth had no idea that Lily and Liam knew each other. She was shocked when Lily saw Liam and exclaimed, "Holy God! It's Saint Crazy! What the hell are you doing in here?"

"I came to see if it was true that no matter how fast you drive a convertible, dogs still can't fly."

"You're so funny, Liam."

"I'm not really funny, but the fact that your dog's name was Lucky? Now that's funny."

"Take gas and die!"

"Hey Lily, you're sober. What happened—bartender die?"

"You're a brat. That's gotta stop."

The judge leaped to her feet and slammed her gavel down, almost breaking her desk in half. The room froze; no one dared move. The judge took a deep breath.

"I don't know what this is all about. Liam, I don't even know who you are right now. I do know that you love helping people. However, if you can't or don't want to do this, that's fine. I'll start the trial procedures."

"No need to, Judge. We're just kidding. Aren't we, Lily?"

"Of course we're kidding, Judge. Hell, our fathers are the best of friends."

"That's news to me, Miss Flowers," said the judge as she sat back down in her leather chair. "Now, Liam, can you do this, or should I remove my ruling?"

"No need to, Amy—I mean, Your Honor. I want to do this. Really."

An hour later, the family attorney, Lily, and Liam left the judge's chambers. They walked outside to the front of the courthouse. Daniel pulled up in the Bentley.

Liam looked at Lily, smiled, and said, "See you in the morning, kiddo."

Lily hopped in the back of the Bentley. As they drove away, Daniel asked, "Who was that guy?"

"My caretaker, the ball-buster."

"Your caretaker? What the hell does that mean?"

"It means my life is over. Please, don't ask. Just drive me home."

Daniel made blueberry pancakes the next morning while Liam and Lily sat out by the pool. They ate the pancakes and talked. Daniel once again wasn't happy. Lily was ignoring him again. It seemed as if he only mattered when no one else was around. After all, Lily was his second chance. He was ready to treat her the way he should have the first time around. He wanted to be in love now. He wanted to be... well, different, but there was always some distraction. He was tired of all this legal business, but figured that if he was going to please the angels and the spirit of the universe, he would have to put up with it. They would see how he had changed and be glad they had given him a second chance. He might even become a legend in heaven. The angels would say to each other 'What a fabulous idea we had.'

He made a fresh pot of coffee and brought it out to the pool. He stopped halfway when he heard Lily and Liam arguing.

"Listen, you're on the waiting list for saints. Maybe *you* wanna save the world, and that's great. But if you think I'm working at one of those shelters, you're crazier than I thought."

"Now, wait a minute. I know you enjoy being a selfish bitch, but you *will* work at a shelter, you *will* pay your debt to society, or you *will* just go to jail—which is really where you belong."

"Do you know who I am? Lily Flowers. That means I give orders, I don't take them."

"Where is your family? Has your father ever been around? Daddy got a million reasons why he can't be here? I'm all you got, kiddo; get used to it."

"Drop dead!"

"That's lovely. I'm done with you. I'll call Amy, and you're on your own. Good luck to you."

As Liam stormed past Daniel, he said, "Find another job, sir. She's going to jail."

Daniel turned the corner to find Lily sitting there smoking.

"Daniel, please, I don't want any coffee right now."

"I figured that. What are you gonna do?"

"Go to trial," she said with a flick of her cigarette.

"Why? You don't have to. Can't you just do this for a year? It'll go fast."

Lily stood up, said nothing, and went over to the pool bar where she made herself a Bloody Mary.

"That's not the answer."

"Daniel, leave me alone. I need to think."

Daniel went and cleaned up the kitchen. He heard the elevator doors open. He put the mop down and ran over to the elevator as the doors closed. He called out and walked around the penthouse. Lily was gone. He took the elevator down to the garage. He found the Bentley still in the parking space. He went to the front desk and asked if they had seen Lily. They told him she had called down and asked for her Mercedes SL500. He had been unaware she still owned one. He ran back to the elevator and took it back up. The doors opened, and there was Faith.

"Truth needs to show you something."

"Tell her not now; I need to get the keys for the Bentley and find Lily."

The next thing Daniel knew, he was sitting in the auditorium.

"Maybe not," Daniel said.

The lights went down, and the projector came on. There was Franco's Deli. Franco Tomonits owned it. It was located on Avenue U and Twenty-eighth Street. Cheese hung over the long chrome deli counter. Slicing machines and scales were behind the counter where the deli men worked. A butcher's block stood in the back of the store and there was sawdust on the floor. It was an old-fashioned Italian market, complete with a bell atop the front door.

As eleven-year-old Nicky Vocci and his father walked up to the deli, Nicky's eyes were aglow. It was December 21, 1957, and Brooklyn looked like the North Pole. A blanket of white snow had fallen. The air was crisp and red and green twinkling lights gave the streets a splendor. As the sounds of Christmas carols and sleigh bells filled the air, the anticipation was almost too much for a young mind to bear.

It was 7:30 p.m., and everyone at Franco's had gone home. Franco was waiting for Joey V. Franco had a gambling problem and owed Joey V ten large. As always, he didn't have it, but he was hoping Joey could wait until after New Year's. The little bell at the front rang.

When Franco saw Joey had brought his son, he had confidence that everything would be all right. He gave Nicky a candy cane, and Joey told his son to wait in the car. The two men walked to the back office. Nicky ate his candy cane, but instead of waiting in the car, he stayed in the deli, looking out the window. Unfortunately, Joey V had come to make an example out of the gambler.

Nicky was looking out the window when he heard Franco scream. Nicky turned around to see the heavyset man running from the back room, bleeding profusely. He yelled out and collapsed on the floor. A knife handle protruded from his chest.

"*Nicky!* Go wait in the car now!" yelled an angry Joey V.

Nicky ran out of the store and to the car. He sat in the front seat, his mind racing. His father got in on the driver's side. He looked at Nicky.

"Son, I told you to go back to the car. But that's neither here nor there. You've just become a man, and that means you didn't see nothing, you know nothing. You just forget about it!"

"Did you kill him, Pop?"

"No. He's fine, but he's hurtin'. Do you know why I had to do that?"

"It doesn't matter, Pop. I'm okay."

"It does matter. I want you to understand. Franco owed me money. I need money to take care of you and your mom and sister. However, he doesn't have it, so that means my family goes without. I can't let that happen. Do you understand?"

"Yeah, I guess so," nodded the boy.

"Can you be a man and do something for me?"

"Anything, Pop. I wanna be a man in your eyes."

"You are a man, son, but you gotta know the cops don't solve crimes—rats do."

"I don't wanna be a rat."

"Of course not; you're Joey V's boy!"

"And I don't do the cops' job for them."

"That's right, Nicky. Hey, how did you get so smart?"

"I'm your son, remember?"

"You're my little man," he said tousling his son's hair. "Hey, Nicky, you play your cards right, maybe one day you can help me."

"I'd like that, Pop," the boy grinned.

"We'll see, Nicky. We'll see."

The pair went out for a hot chocolate, and Joey bought Nicky a new bicycle for two hundred dollars cash. It was a good day.

When school started again that January, Nicky started beating up kids for their lunch money and was soon joined by his pals: Chips and the Hump.

The projector went off, and the lights came up. Truth was sitting right next to Daniel, smiling.

"Can you tell me something?" Daniel asked.

"Sure, what do you want to know?"

"Am I Daniel Peters or Nicky Vocci?"

"Both," replied the angel.

"That's nice."

"You can decide which one you want to be."

"And how's that work?"

"Life is just choice and circumstance. Moments become recollection."

"I don't understand."

"You were eleven years old when your father killed Franco. How many times did you recall that moment? You chose the delusion that Franco deserved to be killed."

"I was a child," he reasoned.

"After that moment, you weren't a child again. You started to fill your soul with hate."

"I didn't know any better!" Daniels argued.

"Oh, come on, Daniel. When you started beating up those children you went to school with, you didn't feel it was wrong? Remember, I am Truth. I can see into your soul."

"Okay, maybe at first, but then—hey, what is this? What do you want from me? Oh, I know—you wanna hear how sorry I am. Well, guess what—it was so long ago I forgot. So now what?"

"Open your heart. Listen to it speak. Become the soul you were meant to be. Let out that piece of the spirit of the universe that lives in each of us."

"What are you talking about?"

"Let's go back to when you started bullying people. What were you, eleven or twelve? Then you got Chips and the Hump involved. And when terrorizing the school wasn't enough, the three of you started stealing cars. Do you remember what happened because of that?"

"I'm dead, and I don't remember nothing!"

"Didn't you go to jail?"

"You mean my father *let* me go to jail."

"Say it!"

"What?" Daniel looked at his shoes.

"How you really felt about your father."

"Who are you, Sigmund Freud? Do you want to know about my penis?"

"Focus! Exactly what happened when you went to jail?"

"Nothing. I went away for six months," he shrugged. "Besides, it was a juvenile center."

"*That* was the turning point," Truth said quietly.

"Why? Because my dad was trying to make me a man?"

"Sorry, I thought he turned his back on you. But I've been wrong before."

Hesitantly, Daniel replied. "No, you're not wrong."

"Tell me what happened."

"Me and the boys started stealing cars. Our dads owned chop shops in Coney. The money was good, so what the hell?"

He continued, "One day the Hump and Chips got pinched. Don Capozzoli gets his lawyers, and *boom*, it never happened. Chips winds up working for his old man. The Hump gets taken in by his old man. I mean, the don is teaching his son. To make a long story short, I get pinched after a car chase.

I also hit one of the cops 'cause he drags me out of the car by my hair. What does *my* old man do? He tells me there's only so many favors he's got... so I get a year. I only spent like five months for good behavior, but I knew what a prick my old man really was. I was his son, and he treated me like the help. After that I spent my time hanging out with the older kids. I learned a lot 'cause I was smarter and meaner than that idiot would ever be."

Daniel paused. "I was sorry when that cop killed him, but I really looked at it as a way to impress the don and then maybe get my own crew. As far as the old man, well, my mother and sister would miss him."

"Daniel, it was then the combative angels took over your ego. Your spirit got smaller as you were shut off from the light."

"So you're saying it wasn't my fault?"

"Let me put it another way. You started thinking wrongly. Then you took negative actions. As a result, your life became negative. In other words, you reap what you sow."

"Wait a minute! Are you saying it's because of the choices I've made?"

"Yes! That's it! Don't you understand choices and consequences?"

"It can't be that simple."

"Ah, but it is."

"So what do I do now?"

"Again, very simple. Start helping instead of hurting. Your will can reconnect with the spirit of the universe, and your soul will heal."

"So that's why you gave me another chance to fall in love?"

"Daniel, there are no second chances. You have to start all over again. You're born, you die, and that's it. If you want a second chance, you must make it happen while you're still alive. You blew all your second chances as Nicky. You're Daniel now, and as Daniel you have other things to do."

"Things like what?"

"Lily and Liam, if they fall in love, have the ability to take new paths in their respective lives. You are here now to make sure that happens."

"She'll never be my Lisa again?"

"That moment has passed into a memory."

Daniel sat back in shock for a very long time. The realization of his wasted life set in. He had put nothing good into his life; therefore, he had gotten nothing good back from it. All his efforts toward amassing money and power meant nothing. He had no real friends and no one to love. And why? Because he had never been a real friend; nor had he loved anyone. Ultimately, he had no real family. No one cared—that is, except Lisa, and he stopped cold when he thought of her. The emptiness of pride and ego had become his only reality. He realized that Truth was merely the unvarnished reflection of whatever anyone had or had not done. Truth could be cold and hard with regard to the reality of his life. And those were the choices he had made.

Daniel turned toward Truth with tears in his eyes and spoke quietly but clearly. "I want to make this right."

"That's all it takes, Daniel. Now go back and help Lily purely for the sake of helping someone."

"Do it and expect nothing in return—am I right?"

"Right. That's what it's all about."

90

Daniel found himself back on Earth, standing in the penthouse kitchen. He called Liam on his cell phone.

"Hello? Liam?"

"Who is this, please?"

"Daniel, Lily's houseman."

"Oh, hi. How can I help you, Daniel?"

"Liam, Lily ran away."

"Of course she did. That's what she always does."

"Help me find her please."

"Why should I?" Liam asked.

"Because I know you care about her and what happens to her."

Liam sighed. "Are you at the penthouse?"

"Yes."

"I'll be right over."

"Thank you." The two men hung up, and Daniel dropped to his knees and cried. He stood up, took a breath, and said out loud to no one in particular, "Let's do this."

❖

The first thing that Liam and Daniel did was track down Brook Stein.

Brook was always Lily's go-to person and she was also the only person on the planet whom Lily truly trusted. They'd found out that Brook was now staying on her father's yacht anchored off Palm Beach. Liam knew that when Brook was on the yacht, she was in the process of drying out. When the two men reached the waterfront, Liam had Daniel wait in the

Bentley. He took the tender out to the yacht. As he boarded the Esquire, he immediately saw Brook lying on the chaise lounge. She was wearing only her sunglasses. Brook spotted Liam and gave him a quick wave. She stood up, stretched out, and put her hands on her hips. She smiled at Liam and then slowly sauntered across the deck and put on her robe.

"When you called, I thought to myself, 'To what do I owe the honor of a visit from the exalted Saint Crazy?'" she said as she sat across from him.

"I'll come right to the point. I'm looking for Lily."

"What else is new?"

"I don't know if you're aware of this, Brook, but Lily is in violation of her probation. She could end up in jail—no joke."

"Oh come now, Liam. Lily Flowers? Daddy wouldn't like that, so it won't happen."

"Brook, this is serious. Do you know what she did?"

"She crashed a car and killed a puppy. This is just another excuse for you to get some of that."

"What is your problem?"

"You're the one with the problem. I know where she is, don't I?"

"I'm not here to play games with you, Brook. Tell me where she is!"

"Yelling. You're yelling. I'll put it to you this way…" she paused. "She's not banging my brother as of late. Oh, I'm sorry. I guess you didn't know that."

"Lily's dating Heath?" Liam stared off in the distance.

"More like getting it on with him. Liam, it's hard for a girl to say 'I love you' when her mouth is full."

"You're a pig, Brook, you always were. That's why I ain't interested."

"I am a pig, little boy, and I'd like to make you a man. So I've got a deal for you."

"What foolish idea is this?"

"Actually, it's brilliant."

"What is it? Tell me."

"I'll tell you where Lily is, and you take me out. I'm a good woman, Liam, and I want you. And I always get what I want."

"You are the most self-centered and stupid woman I have ever met."

"Oh, come on, Liam. It's just one little date. Let's get to know each other."

Liam stood up, took a deep breath, and controlled his anger. He turned away and walked back to the tender. As he boarded, Brook called out his name. Liam looked up to see her sitting on the yacht railing with her legs wide open, giggling.

"See anything you like?"

Liam looked away, speechless. He got back in the Bentley and slammed the door. Daniel looked at him confused.

"Daniel, please just take me home!"

"Take you home? Where's Lily? What's going on?"

"Lily and her little psycho bitch friend Brook are playing manipulative games. I, for one, refuse to play along."

"What games?"

"In a nutshell, Brook wants a date or she won't tell me where Lily is." Daniel shook his head and, laughing to himself, looked into the rearview mirror.

"Yo, tell me something, hotshot. Is it the money that —— you rich morons up or what? Lily's in trouble, and you have to go out on a date and then we can find Lily. What's the problem? Take the bitch out for a steak. You've got the cash. You might even get lucky."

"It's not the cash. I date whomever I want, and believe me, Daniel, I have no interest in getting lucky."

"You have no interest in getting lucky? Can I have your man card?"

"Excuse me?"

"You stay here; I'll be right back," Daniel said as he exited the Bentley, hopped onto the tender, and motored over to the yacht. Fifteen minutes later, he was back in the car.

"Good news. Lily's in New York, and you've got a date with Brook Saturday night. Well, now that's done. I guess we gotta go to New York, but we need to get there quickly."

"I'll call Boca Airport. My plane will be ready in an hour."

"You're the best, Mr. Patrick."

"Call me Liam."

"Thanks, Liam, that's nice of you."

"I don't feel superior just because I'm rich. I was born into it. But I will not date Brook."

"It's a dirty job, but you gotta do it, and if you sleep with her, I'll still respect you."

"I can't believe you told her I'd go out with her."

"No, I didn't say that."

"Then why did she tell you where Lily was?"

"'Cause I told her I knew exactly where her brother was. She looked worried. It was then that I informed her you had accepted her invitation for a date, so to speak."

"Why would she care if you knew where her brother was?"

"Why don't you ask her Saturday night?"

"Thanks, I guess I will."

"Good, now let's go get Lily and stop this."

The two men flew to New York. During the two-hour flight, Liam thought to himself, *Who is this young man? He's like no other houseman I've ever met. He exudes superiority; one instinctively can't say no to him. He looks young, yet he speaks and acts a person well beyond his years. He's like an old-time mobster, yet I don't feel anything sinister from him. He seems like a good man. Come to think of it, where did he come from?* Liam kept going over these thoughts again and again in his head.

As the limo sped into Manhattan, he almost forgot why they were on their way there. He knew Mr. Flowers's people would have vetted him thoroughly before employing him. But I don't know. *There's just something about him.*

Lily laid on the floor, watching the room spin, an empty quart of vodka next to her. She thought about how no one cared about her. Mom and Dad didn't want her. Men only seemed to want one thing. Her eyes filled with tears and she wished she could die. The front doorbell ringing rapidly interrupted Lily's self-pity. *Ding-dong. Ding-dong. Ding-dong.* She got to her feet somehow and staggered to the door.

"Who is it?" she hollered from behind the door.

"Open the door!"

"Dannyboy? How did you find me?"

Lily pulled the front door open, and there stood Daniel. He pushed past her into the penthouse. He was angry yet relieved that she was alive and in one piece.

"Look at you. It's two o'clock in the afternoon, and you're wasted!" he said

"Oh, save it, Dannyboy. Let's get a drink together. What do you like to drink? Let's get started; you've got some catching up to do."

"Lily, you can barely stand; you've had enough."

"Oh, kiss my tits! Chill, DB; have a drink. Hey, 'DB' sounds cool; what do you think?"

"Don't ask me to have a drink again. I'm here to take you home."

"Home? That's for people who have people—know what I mean?"

"Yes, I do, Lily. I really do."

"Good. 'Cause I don't."

The front door opened, and in walked Liam. He stood there glaring at Lily and then Daniel. Lily stood and swayed slowly back and forth.

"Nice, Daniel. This is what I flew up here to save?"

"Easy there, Liam."

"She's a preferable pain in the behind; and you, Daniel, are a pain in the front, if you know what I mean."

"Yeah, yeah, I break your balls."

As the two men went back and forth, Lily collapsed onto the floor. Her houseman scooped her up in his arms as Liam ran to the kitchen for ice. Daniel was pleasantly surprised at the strong body the angels had given him. He easily laid her on the couch as though he were a prince in a fairytale. Liam came out of the kitchen with an ice pack. He moved Daniel out of the way, sat on the couch, and put the cold compress on Lily's head.

He looked at Daniel and said, "I know how to handle a drunk."

Lily sprang up suddenly and threw up in Liam's lap. Daniel roared with laughter, infuriating Liam.

"That's it! Good luck, 'Dannyboy'. I'm gone."

"Liam, sir, I'm sorry I laughed. After all, there's nothing funny about this. Sir, you can't leave like this. At least let me wash your clothes."

Liam stood staring at Daniel and then said, "She must really be important to you. I mean, you make a bad attempt at kissing my ass. Like you're really gonna wash my clothes. Like I'd ever even wear this outfit again."

"Okay, Liam, listen to me. First, it's puke, not battery acid. Second, there's the master bedroom. I'm sure there's one of those big fluffy robes in there. You put on the robe; I'll throw your clothes in the washer and dryer. Third, we get her back to Florida before the courts find out she left, and Judge Amy doesn't have to know you failed."

"I failed?"

"Are you not in charge of her rehabilitation?"

"Daniel, do my feelings concern you at all?"

"I said I'd wash your clothes. I'll even make lunch. Please, Liam. Help me!"

"All right, I'll stay and help. But I don't know how Florida is not gonna find out. Do you really think you're gonna get away with this?"

"Oh, please, this is nothing. Try hiding a dead body." Daniel wished he could have caught the words, but they'd already been released. Liam had a puzzled look on his face. "Oh, come on, Liam, I'm kidding. Can't you tell?"

Liam said nothing but rather turned and walked into the bedroom. He took off his clothes and threw them onto the living room floor. He hopped into the shower. As the water began pelting his body, he thought, *Who is this guy? He was serious about hiding a dead body.* Liam couldn't put his finger on it, but somehow Daniel was familiar. That was what really bothered him. Somehow he knew him from somewhere. *Impossible!* Whatever it was, Liam was determined to find out.

When Liam walked back into the living room, Lily was sitting up on the couch, sipping coffee. Daniel rushed into the room carrying pizza boxes. He also had a six-pack of Coke.

"Chow time, gang. One has mushrooms, the other pepperoni. Dig in."

At 10:00 p.m. that night, Liam's private jet landed at Boca Airport. Liam hopped into a limo and went home. Daniel took a hung-over Lily to the Excalibur Penthouse and put her to bed. Daniel went to his bed. He lay there thinking, *How am I gonna get two people who were enemies to fall in love? And how could I help someone and expect nothing?*

Meanwhile, Liam lay in his bed, wondering who Daniel reminded him of.

Liam had finished his workout. He sat on the beach in meditation, but he was having trouble concentrating. He couldn't get Lily off his mind. Everyone who was supposed to love Lily had let her down but Lily sucked it up and was touched. She was bright and beautiful, something special. Somehow she had become insecure, and then came the drinking and drugs. The party girl became promiscuous. As time went on, the arrests came. Hell, the previous year she had gotten into a knife fight in Miami. Now she had killed a dog and gotten a DUI. Lily was going nowhere fast. She had even hooked up with Heath Stein. Heath had gotten Lily into the pills and coke. *Yeah, Heath Stein, real tough guy.* Liam had loved Lily from the first time he saw her. He didn't care what she had done; he wanted her to straighten up and become the fabulous person she was born to be. Liam prayed, asking God to help him help Lily.

Lily had been getting sick to her stomach all morning. Daniel made her tea and toast and brought it out to the pool. Lily sat at the shallow end, her head pounding.

"You look good, kid," Daniel said.

"Really?"

"Yeah. When are they burying you?"

"Daniel, don't tease me. I feel like crap."

"Don't drink a quart of vodka, and you might have better mornings."

Suddenly tears welled up in Lily's eyes. "Daniel, you're an answer to my prayers."

Daniel looked surprised.

"I prayed to God," she continued. "I asked him to show me he cares. And he sent me you. I know it 'cause you really care about me. I can't believe you came all the way to New York to get me."

"Aren't you forgetting someone?"

"You mean Saint Crazy?"

"His name is Liam Patrick, so stop 'Saint Crazy,' will ya?"

"Why, Daniel, I had no idea you cared."

"I got work to do."

"Wait, Daniel; I'm sorry."

"No, Lily, you wait! Let me explain something to you. He used all his resources. He was the one who found you—not me. All he had to do was call the judge and be done with it. So the next time you're thanking God for me, you might want to thank Him for Liam, too. Remember: it's my job to keep you safe. He did it because he cares."

"I didn't realize that."

"There's a lot of stuff you don't realize. He even let that bitch Brook blackmail him into a date. That's why she told us where you were. So if your life stinks, get your head out of your ass and stop hanging out with fools."

Lily didn't like being talked to that way, but she respected Daniel enough to listen.

"I'm not trying to be mean, kid," Daniel sad softer. "I just want what's best for you. I'm gonna make lunch. You think about what I said."

Lily sat there, her head spinning. She realized Daniel was right. Liam was a good man. She decided that maybe she should change her attitude toward him.

She called Liam to thank him. During their conversation, something marvelous happened. All the strife between them melted away. Liam and Lily let their guards down, and without those walls, a bond formed. And as small as it was, a spark started, but with love that's all you need.

Out of the blue, Liam found himself saying, "I have to go on a date with Brook though. May I see you afterward?"

"Why are you going if you don't want to?"

"I gave my word."

"Well then, Liam, I would like that."

"That's great! How about coffee at the club?"

"Okay, what time?"

"Nine o'clock. Good for you?"

"I'll see you then."

"Lily, I'm looking forward to it."

"Are you sure? I mean, you're not gonna change your mind and go off with Brook?"

"Brook? You don't have to worry about that. I'm allergic to baby food."

Lily laughed and then said, "I'll see you at nine, Liam. Goodbye for now."

Lily hung up the phone and pressed her fingers to her lips. She thought about how people look all around for happiness when most of the time it's right in front of them.

❖

After Liam hung up, he pumped his fist in the air. "Yes!" he exclaimed.

❖

Daniel brought lunch out to Lily. Lily was gleaming from head to toe.

"God help me, I got a date with Liam tonight!"

"A date? How did that happen?"

"Daniel, it was nuts! I called Liam to thank him. The next thing I know, I'm flirting with him. Then he starts flirting with me and—*bang*—a date comes up! Thank you, Daniel!"

"For what? It's just tuna sandwiches," he teased.

"For being you, silly. You have great advice and an interesting way of giving it."

"Eat your lunch."

"Lunch! I have to call my hairdresser, my couturier, my..."

"Yeah, yeah. After you eat, got it?"

"Daniel, you know I'm your boss."

"I got work to do, so come on—more eating, less talking."

"Okay, boss."

Daniel cleaned up after lunch while Lily made her phone calls. His heart felt like an anvil. He knew there was no more Lisa. All he had left was pain.

After cleaning the kitchen, Daniel went outside and stood on the terrace. He looked out at the ocean below as a gull skimmed along the sea. Daniel watched that bird and thought about how it didn't have a care in the world. He wondered if a human being could ever feel like that.

Faith appeared behind him. "Hey you!" she said.

"Hey."

"Could you turn around and acknowledge me?" the angel asked.

"Okay, you're acknowledged. Anything else I can do?"

"Aw, I'm sorry, Daniel. Are you having a pity party? Should I come back in a couple years? Is it me, or did you put yourself in this predicament?"

"Oh good, you're in the mood to give me a speech!"

"I'm in the mood to give you a kick in the ass."

"Did you want something?" he replied impatiently.

"As a matter of fact, I wanted to show you something. But now I don't know if I'm going to."

"You got something to show me?"

"I knew that would get your attention. I mean, heaven knows it's all about you."

"You know, I thought helping the woman I love fall for another man was bad. I thought it couldn't get any worse. But I was wrong. In my depression, I forgot that an angel would be breaking my balls. So why don't you send me to hell? I'm not the man or the soul or whatever it is you want me to be, 'cause it seems to me that hell is a lot easier."

"You're right; it would be easier. But the answer is no. And besides, you've already saved Lily."

"What the —— are you talking about?"

"You saved Lily's life."

"You mean she's gonna fall in love with Liam. She's on the road she's supposed to be on."

"No, nothing like that, but it's a start."

"So how did I save her life? You just said Lily just made a start."

Faith handed Daniel the New York Daily News. The headline read, "Heiress Leaps to Death in Manhattan" in bold

103

black-and-white. The chronicle was dated the same day Liam and Daniel found Lily.

"That's what Lily went to Manhattan to do, and she would've if you hadn't stopped her. And by the way, you helped a lot of other souls too."

"How?"

"She would have landed in the middle of Central Park East. There would have been a major car pileup. Four innocent people would have died. Two teenage boys would have observed her fall. Their youth would have died. They would have started to experiment with drugs. They would have become addicts and criminals. The families and friends of the four that were killed—they would have become angry. Countless people would have believed life unfair, including the millions who read the story in the news or saw it on TV. In New York alone, eight million people would be left thinking that if a rich, beautiful heiress couldn't find happiness, how could they? And as for Lily, her soul would have fallen right into Insecurity's arms and Pride's mad realm. Pride and his combative angels are at their best when humankind is confused. You changed history and stopped all that. All it took was a simple act of caring. Think about that the next time you feel sorry for yourself."

"I feel dizzy."

"It's amazing but simple. Every single act of kindness multiplies itself toward peace on Earth." The two stood silent while staring at each other, and then Faith said, "Just believe in me."

"I'm starting to. I want to."

"That's great, Daniel, 'cause I have some bad news."

"Go ahead, tell me."

"Insecurity will be on his way. He'll want to know what happened to his plan."

"And...?"

"You'll be able to see him. But remember to act as if you don't. Don't let him figure out who you are."

"And when should I expect him?"

"I don't know exactly."

"That's nice, just what I need, a psycho angel coming after me. Know what? Maybe we'll become buddies. I know— I'll take him bowling."

"I don't think he bowls."

"I guess destroying souls takes up most of his day. I mean, what am I worried about? It's only the battle of good and evil. Mankind, the world—nothing to lose sleep over."

"Are you done?"

"Yeah, pretty much."

"You'll be fine. We wouldn't ask you to do something you couldn't handle. Now go help Lily get ready for her date."

"Ready for her date? I can hear me saying it now: Sorry I sent the world to hell, God, but didn't Lily's ensemble look superb?"

"Have a little trust. Just go help Lily; it will take your mind off things. I'm here for you; always remember that. Daniel, I'm very proud of you." And with that, Faith disappeared.

Daniel called out after her, "Let's just hope her shoes match her purse."

❖

Insecurity lay on the ground, listening to the conversation Anger and Pride were having.

"I loved that beating you gave him. You think it was enough?" Pride asked.

"He didn't fight back, the lazy bastard. I hate when they just take the beating. But then again, I hate everything!"

"Bravo!"

"May I ask you something?"

"Feel free."

"The soul you call Lily Flowers—it's only her second birth. What I mean is, she's a screw-up. Even if she lives, she really won't matter. She'll just die alone and drunk. So why push Insecurity so hard to get her to kill herself? I don't really care about her; I just want to know why all the urgency."

"Oh, my angry brother, let me tell you the whole story. For the last 250 years, the spirit of the universe has had one soul reborn again and again and again. It turns out that ever since this soul was called into being, no matter what skin he was put into, he helped his fellow human beings. This soul is powerful—full of courage, wisdom, and integrity. We have not been able to shake him. Anyway, the most recent time, he was put into Lisa Stein's womb. If he had been born, the love Nicky and Lisa had for him would have saved them. They would have run away to Australia and started all over again, this time on the right track. But Fear got to Nicky, and he killed Lisa, the baby, and his only chance. Or so we thought."

"Then he saved that woman's life, and Faith took his soul." "Exactly. So now we go to plan B."

"Which is?"

"Insecurity planted his seeds in her mind long ago. So she parties, sleeps around, looks for love and self-worth—the usual. But now that those angels have our soul, we have to step it up a notch."

"Let me guess—Insecurity puts so much doubt in her she takes her own life. Then we get her soul."

"Very good! That's it. What you may not know is, I plan to offer that soul to Nicky. He comes out of hiding then we get both souls."

"And wouldn't that be a feather in your cap."

"Yes, it would, but the cherry on top is the soul that keeps coming back to help. As Liam Patrick, he'll go through life heartbroken, and when his life on Earth is over, maybe this time he will give up on humans and not come back."

"It's brilliant!"

"It all starts with the self-destruction of Lily Flowers."

As Anger and Pride began to walk off, Pride knelt down and whispered into Insecurity's ear, "Fill her with doubt; do whatever it takes. But I want that soul."

Insecurity lay there for a moment. Suddenly he sprang up into a sitting position. A light bulb came on—an idea. She hadn't jumped to her death in New York. Why was that? Because of that houseman. He had saved her; she trusted him. How could she lose that trust? *She must feel alone in the world. What if he seduced her? What if she fell in love with him instead of Liam? Then he would show his false motive. If she found out that all he wanted was sex, she would be destroyed. Liam would be heartbroken. He wouldn't want anything to do with her. Maybe one would kill the other. The survivor would go to jail.* Insecurity jumped to his feet and smiled. "This could work," he said aloud.

❖

Brook called Liam to inform him she was going to London. It seemed Heath had run into one of Brook's old flames, who had told Heath how much he missed Brook. He liked to party and was good in bed, so Brook figured, *What the hell? Why not?*

Liam could hardly wait to get off the phone. As soon as he and Brook ended their conversation, he called Lily with the good news. Brook had cancelled; it was now an official date.

After Liam hung up with Lily, he called his barber and tailor. A haircut and a new suit were needed. He took a cab to his tailor so his BMW convertible could be detailed. Then he made one last phone call: reservations at Nero's Fiddle.

Lily's closet was stripped bare. Out of the hundreds of outfits, she had nothing to wear. Daniel was half-crazed and exhausted. Lily had Daniel drive her to the dressmaker, and then Daniel went and picked up Lily's hairdresser and manicurist. He drove them to the penthouse and made them lunch. An hour later, Lily showed up with her dressmaker. The penthouse sounded like a henhouse on steroids. Daniel was amazed at how four women could all talk at the same time and still understand what each other were saying.

The time arrived. Lily went downstairs to meet Liam. She looked stunning with her hair pulled back into a ponytail, showing off her caramel-brown eyes. She wore a white miniskirt suit that showed off her long tan legs punctuated with white high heels. She walked across the floor and into the elevator. She was light-footed and elegant. Like a light breeze, she came and was gone.

The penthouse was now as quiet as a morgue. But unlike the undertaker's mortuary, it looked as if Bloomingdale's had exploded. Daniel was going to spend Saturday night putting the place back together. The full moon looked luxurious as it lit the dark ocean below it. Liam and Lily stood on the pier, holding hands. Fingers locked, their hair swayed with the ocean breeze.

"What a night," Liam said.

Lily turned and faced him. "Custom made for us, babe."

"Babe? I thought I was Saint Crazy."

"Shut up and kiss me, you fool." The two shared a smile followed by a long, passionate kiss.

Daniel was sweating, his back and knees aching. The bathroom alone had taken two hours to clean. He had also put the closet back together. There were 175 pairs of shoes. Daniel thought to himself, *she has two feet and 175 pairs of shoes.* Daniel wasn't sure what was worse—putting back all the shoes or counting them.

All that was left to do was mop the floors. Daniel went into the washroom and began filling up a bucket with Pine-Sol and hot water. He heard a noise from the living room. He turned off the faucet and listened. He couldn't hear anything over his heartbeat. The penthouse was silent, so Daniel went about his chores. He began to mop the kitchen floor; then the sound of the terrace door opening destroyed the silence.

"Hello!" Daniel yelled out.

Putting the mop down, he walked into the living room. The curtains by the sliding doors blew in the breeze. Daniel walked over and shut the door; then he heard footsteps in Lily's room. He walked gingerly toward Lily's bedroom. Just then, the mop came flying into the living room. Daniel stood frozen and desperate.

"Liam, Lily! Stop messing around, guys!" he called out.

Daniel stood for a moment, scared and confused. The utter stillness started to close in. He shook it off. He walked over to pick up the mop. Just then, Faith leaped from the kitchen.

"Boo!"

Daniel leaped back, screaming and even wetting himself.

"What the —— is wrong with you? Are you insane or just trying to kill me? Goddamn it, I peed my pants!"

"Stop screaming. First off, don't say God you-know-what. It's very negative. Second, you died four years ago."

"I died four years ago, so you can't kill me. How about this?"

"I don't have a vagina."

"'I don't have a vagina,' she says." And with that, Daniel collapsed on the floor crying.

Faith took him in her arms until he stopped sobbing. When Daniel regained his composure, Faith said, "I'm not trying to scare you, but you called out. If I were Insecurity, I'd have just found Pride's soul; then I'd have the combative angels descend on you. Lily would not be saved, Liam would not find true love, and you would be a lost soul in Pride's mad realm. Is that what you want?"

"No, but how can I do this?"

110

"When you were Nicky Vocci, you never showed emotion. You acted like all that killing didn't bother you—like killing Lisa was nothing. To the outside world, you were cold and tough. Ignoring the fact that you were hurting inside, you buried how you felt until you couldn't feel anymore. Maybe that's why you saved that woman. Don't you see? All humans are angels. You just have trouble letting all that good out. It's easier to have pride. And that's because it's not real. It's not who you really are, but you believe in that illusion. And that's how you lose your soul. But now that can be a good thing. Please act like you can't see or hear Insecurity, like Nicky Vocci would. Act like you were born Daniel Peter, not Nicky Vocci's lost soul hiding in Daniel Peter's body. You can do it; I know you can."

Daniel sat on the floor, looking at the little angel with the big blue eyes. He put his head on her shoulder and cried.

After Daniel pulled himself together, Faith helped him with the floors. Faith left, and then Daniel got undressed and went to bed. It was 9:00 p.m.

Liam and Lily couldn't stop kissing. It was as if they were teenagers all over again. They stopped long enough to take a ride to Starbucks for some coffee.

"This date would have never happened if not for Daniel," Liam said.

"You got that right, babe."

"You've been hanging out with Daniel too long." The two laughed. "Lily, who is he? Where did your father find him?"

111

"I don't know. I never really asked. It's like he dropped out of the sky."

"Lily, do you know about my interest in true crime?"

"No. In fact, I don't even care about your interest in true crime."

"Hey, wait a minute. What's with all that anger?"

"I think you're gonna say something bad about Daniel. I don't want to hear it. He saved my life."

"No, you're wrong."

"You weren't asking me where he came from because you think he's one of those mobsters you get so excited about?"

"Not because he is one, but because he reminds me of one."

"Liam, keep it to yourself. I love and trust Daniel. He's my only real friend, and I like having a real friend."

"He's my friend too. Remember: we both went to New York."

"You went because he made you."

"Lily, please, I don't want to fight. Can we drop it?"

"Then why did you bring it up?"

"Because I'm stupid."

"Forget the coffee. I need a drink. Let's go to the Irish cottage."

"Lily, I'm really sorry. Can't we just sit here and talk?"

Lily got up and walked down the block and around the corner. Liam just sat there sipping at his coffee. He hung his head back and said aloud, "Nice going!"

Daniel lay in bed, staring at the TV. Suddenly Insecurity flew in through the ceiling. The dwarfish creature had yellow eyes, dark hair, and an orange beak. Insecurity landed on the bed at Daniel's feet. Daniel's mouth went dry as he slammed his eyes shut.

"Don't move; don't move; don't move," he repeated to himself over and over again. The combative angel walked up his torso.

His black wings pricked at Daniel's legs. Insecurity stood on Daniel's chest and put his beak into Daniel's ear. Between the torture and pain, Daniel passed out.

Daniel came to and found he was alone. His legs were gashed and bruised. The air in the room was stale and dank. Daniel started screaming at the top of his lungs. Faith flew in and picked the screaming Daniel up in her arms. They flew back through the ceiling and into the auditorium. Once there, Daniel sat in shock, staring into space. Faith sat next to him, holding his hand.

Liam had his forehead on the table. He sat back up. There was Lily, coming back around the corner. He got to his feet, and Lily eased up to him.

"Which mobster does Daniel remind you of?" she asked cordially.

"A guy named Nicky Vocci. I thought you were gone."

"I changed my mind, Liam."

"Thank you for coming back."

"Don't thank me, babe. I realized there's nothing in the Irish Cottage for me."

"Lily, I don't know what to say." Lily sat back down and crossed her legs. "Do tell. Who's Nicky Vocci?" Lily purred.

Liam told Lily the history of the Capozzoli family.

Lily endeavored to act interested, but eventually said, "Stop, Liam, please. It's too much information."

"Sorry, Lily, I get carried away. These people fascinate me."

"Yeah, psycho felons get me wet."

"Okay, I get the point."

"Babe, I still don't see how Daniel reminds you of that Nick Whack person."

"Knick Knack," Liam corrected.

"Whatever."

"I got my hands on an old TV news show. Back in 1990 in New York's Superior Court, Nicky Vocci was on trial for racketeering. Anyway, he's on the way out of the courtroom and stops to talk to a reporter. He looks right at the camera and says, 'They put me on trial without proof. What the —— , did we move to Russia?'"

"You're losing me, Liam."

"Lily, Daniel sounds just like Nicky when he says, 'What the freak.' And his eyes have that same look. That same look in his eyes Daniel has when he gets mad."

"Okay, babe, time to change the subject."

"Am I upsetting you?"

"This is a stupid conversation."

"You wanna talk football?"

"No."

"Baseball?"

"Liam, stop being silly," Lily said, smirking.

"May I have one of those kisses, Miss Lily?" Liam said in a southern drawl. Lily laughed, got up, and sat on Liam's lap. The two began kissing.

❖

Back in the auditorium, Daniel had run onto the stage. He collapsed, rolled into a ball, and began rocking back and forth.

"I can't do it ... can't do it ... can't do it ..."

He repeated this over and over. Faith stood over him, not knowing what to do. Suddenly the exit doors flew open, and Truth and the rest of the angels flew in. As always, Truth took command of the situation.

"Ladies, we have to act fast. Daniel is full of Insecurity. Grace, Serenity, get the gurney. Humility, Acceptance, help me get him up."

The angels got Daniel up and laid him on the gurney. Daniel began to scream and thrust. The gurney tipped over and crashed to the floor. Daniel tried to get up and run, but Truth grabbed him by the legs. The two were grappling on the floor; Daniel's anxiety was turning into hysteria. Truth called out, "Can someone give me a hand please?"

Working together, the angels finally restrained Daniel. Faith gave him an examination. During her inspection, she was able to find the seeds Insecurity had planted in Daniel's ear. Having been in the slightest contact with Faith, the insecurity disappeared, and Daniel stopped and laid still, the angels on top of him.

"What the freak is this? If you ladies want some, all you have to do is ask."

"Want some what?" the angels responded in unison.

"Oh, brother!"

"Okay, ladies, it's over. Let's get up now," Truth said.

Liam's BWM made a left from A1A into his driveway, past the batting cages, and up to the front door. He walked around the car and opened the door for Lily. Her dainty feet lifted her out of the car. Although Lily was refined, she couldn't help exclaiming "Holy crap" when she saw Liam's house.

Hurricane Wilma had destroyed the original family mansion. Liam's father gave it to Liam, and Liam had it completely demolished. Then he had built a glass igloo. It was made out of black hurricane glass. From the inside, you could see out; but from the outside, you couldn't see in. Lily stood in jaw-dropping amazement.

"What do you think?" Liam asked.

"Babe, you're one of a kind. I heard people say that you lived in a house shaped like an igloo, but until you see it ..."

"That's why they call me Saint Crazy."

"Liam, you own the only igloo in South Florida."

"You think?"

"Well, babe, can I see the inside please?"

"But of course, my dear."

The two lovers entered the house.

Lily stood in the foyer, confused. There was a giant empty room. The marble floors made it look like a frozen lake. She turned around to see Liam standing by what looked like a fuse box. He began pushing buttons, and a giant flat-screen TV dropped from the ceiling. A round bed came up from the floor. and spun around, revealing a full bar. Track lighting illuminated the room.

"Ta-da!" Liam exclaimed.

"Wow, babe. How much did all this cost?"

"Millions, Lily, millions. But to me it's worth it."

"Babe, all I see is a bar and that giant bed. I don't see any place to sit and talk, and I assure you that's all I'm here for."

"Wait a second, young lady; don't get the wrong idea."

"I'm just telling you what's gonna happen and what's not gonna happen."

"Don't get excited. My only plan was to sit out on the deck and have some wine and cheese."

"You still have that dock that goes out into the ocean?"
"The only thing I changed was the mansion. I still have the deck and the pool. I still own the beach. I just needed a place to eat and sleep when I'm down here, so I built this igloo. All it really is, is a bedroom and a kitchen. The kitchen is right through that door. The other door on the left is a bathroom. Nice and simple. I don't need the housekeepers—the maids. Just groundskeepers twice a month and, of course, the pool man."

"What happened to the tennis court?"

"Batting cages."

"Nice, Liam."

"Well, shall we?"

"Let's go, I love that deck."

The dock began at the house and went from the beach out over the ocean about a hundred feet. It ended in a gazebo. Lily sat in the gazebo, sipping at her glass of white wine.

"So, Liam, how many conquests have you had here?"

"A lot. This place is a real panty dropper."

"Liam!"

"You asked."

"Is that why I'm here?"

"If I said it never crossed my mind, I'd be lying. However, one-night stands used to be enough; now it's kind of boring. I don't know; I just feel I want more."

"That's funny, babe, I've been feeling the same way, especially after what happened with that pig, Heath."

"What happened with Heath?"

Lily sat, shrinking. She had thought Liam knew. Now came the awkward silence. Lily didn't want Liam to hear it from someone else. Embarrassing as it was, she told him the story. Much to her surprise, Liam took hold of her hand. He looked into her eyes, and there was no awkwardness. He listened with patience and compassion.

"That's not your fault. You were trying to please your boyfriend. I can't stand people who take advantage."

"Liam, he wasn't my boyfriend. He was my buddy."

"Lily, you know how I date older women?"

"Yeah, so?"

"So the reason is that most of them just want sex. I used to think, 'Give me a forty-year-old divorcee who just wants to have some fun.' So you see, we're not so different. We're both trying to fill our own emptiness."

"Banging our heads against the wall, babe."

"Our heads as well as other parts."

They both laughed. Liam kissed Lily gently on the lips. The two took their chairs and put them next to each other. They sat watching the ocean in a comfortable silence.

Two hours later, Liam took Lily home. Lily felt lighter than air when she stepped off the elevator and went wafting into her room. She got undressed and climbed into bed. She noticed Daniel had put clean sheets on her bed as she curled up and thanked God for the men in her life.

Faith put Nicky's soul back into Daniel. Daniel lay on his bed, staring at the ceiling. That's how he would spend the rest of the night.

Sunday morning, Lily made Daniel breakfast. The rest of the day was uneventful. Daniel listened over and over again to Lily rambling about Liam and the date. Lily couldn't have known about the lump in Daniel's throat or the heaviness in his heart.

❖

Megan Brunstien graduated from the University of Chicago with a law degree at twenty-three. At the age of twenty-four, she became an associate at Strenger & Sommers, a prestigious Chicago law firm. Megan was a blond version of Lily—five feet six with long, shapely legs and a full bosom. Megan's life was bright and full of success. But then her youth and bad decisions betrayed her. Megan had just turned thirty-eight, and now she must start life anew and leave behind the smoldering train wreck her life had become.

Ten years before, Megan had a love affair. The object of her affection was Phil Sommers, Jr., the son of Phil Sommers, Sr. Phil was the son of a CEO and was tall, smart, and ostentatious. He was everything a girl would want. Just ask his wife. Two years had come and gone, and still Megan waited for Phil's divorce. That summer, Megan came out of the shadows. She went into CEO Phil Sommers Sr.'s office, told him of the affair, and congratulated him on becoming a grandfather. And, of course, she informed him of the impending lawsuit.

Megan never filed a lawsuit; she just got an abortion, along with five million dollars and a condo in Battery Park City on the West Side of Manhattan. So off to New York City Megan went, all guilty parties absolved. Phil, Jr. was very grateful that daddy had been able to fix it. He never realized Megan had stopped taking her birth control pills on purpose. What Megan didn't know was that Lust and Suspicion were escorting her over to Fear and Anger. They would leave her life in shambles. Then Insecurity would destroy whatever faith she had. Then the demon would finish the job, and Pride would finally have Megan's soul.

It all started in New York City for Megan. With money, a posh condo, and a new boyfriend, she was on top of the world. He was built like a Greek statue and the passion made Megan dizzy. Three weeks after they met, he moved in. Megan started her own law practice, and she worked long hours. Her boyfriend said he was a personal trainer, but to Megan and everyone else it seemed he didn't do much. Within a year, the relationship had become volatile. It ended with the brutality of Megan stabbing him. This time Megan lost everything, including her freedom. Because of a plea bargain, she got five to ten years. Her background put her in a minimum-security prison. She was on her best behavior and got probation. After four and a half years, she was going to take part in a program program started by Liam Patrick and prison officials. The Prodigal Sons & Daughters Welcome Back Program was for model prisoners. Upon receiving probation, they went to live in a halfway community for a year. Once there, they would receive counseling and job training, and they would then reenter society and, it was hoped, flourish. Thanks to this program, 75 percent of the men and women who graduated made it.

What had started out as two small communities in upstate New York now spanned the entire East Coast. Many men and women volunteered for the Big Brother and Sister Outreach Program. Most were graduates. They befriended the new parolees and took them shopping or to the movies. They showed them that it worked and, most of all, gave them hope.

Lily and Megan had a lot in common. They were both intelligent, beautiful, and suicidal. Lily had community service to do, so Liam had Megan placed in Florida. Liam hoped the two would become friends and help each other. Maybe together they'd become one normal person.

Megan read Cosmo on the plane as she was on her way to Prodigal Sons & Daughters in Florida.

Monday morning, Daniel drove Lily to Prodigal Sons & Daughters. It was hidden off the Dixie Highway in Delray. Wrought-iron gates kept the women secure and the rest of the world out. The community was a well-arranged cul-de-sac where six townhouses formed a circle. Five of the townhouses were residence domiciles each housing four parolees. The sixth townhouse was for offices, therapy, and job training. At any given time, there were twenty-five women there trying to put their lives back on track.

Lily stood in Liam's office, looking out the window. She watched as some women scuttled about. Still others stayed in groups, smoking cigarettes. She wondered what she had done to deserve this. She hadn't meant to get that drunk or kill Lucky. After all, the damages were paid for. She had lost her dog. Not only that, but the media had reported it. She was on the eleven o'clock news, her misdeeds recorded for posterity. But here she was, doing community service. Lily walked over to a chair and sat down. She started feeling depressed. A spinning sensation came over her. She put her head in her hands. Liam walked in.

"Lily, are you all right? Why are you trembling?" Liam kneeled before her and held her hands.

"Babe, please get me out of here," she said.

"I can't, sweetie; you have to do this. I made a deal with Judge Amy."

"Oh please! Can't we just pay Judge Amy?"

"Lily, don't get irrational. You can't buy your way out of everything."

Lily pushed her chair back and got to her feet. She began to rub her hands and pace back and forth. "What's the point of being rich if you can't do what you want?"

"Calm down, sweetie."

"Babe, sorry, I'm calling Daniel and going home. You wanna help these people, knock yourself out. I don't want to help them, talk to them, or be around them. You're Saint Crazy, babe; this is your thing."

"You are these people. Money can't cleanse your soul."

"Oh, Liam, you're so deep. You're right, I'll do it. You saved me; now I want to change the world."

"I don't need your sarcasm. I went to a lot of trouble. I got the judge to give you community service. I had Megan transferred down here so you could do your community service. So if you want to go home, I'll call the judge and tell her."

"Don't threaten me!"

"It's not a threat; it's a promise."

Lily realized Liam wasn't giving in. She had no choice.

A half hour later, Megan arrived. Lily was taken aback by how pretty she was. The two women went into Liam's office for a meet and greet. Megan wanted out of Prodigal Sons & Daughters. Lily wanted to go home. But it didn't matter; both were compelled to make the best of the situation.

"How was the flight?" Lily asked.

"Good."

"I bet you're glad you're out of prison."

"I'm still in prison."

"Megan—may I call you Megan?—it's gonna be all right."

"Call me what you like, but don't tell me it's gonna be all right. I'm tired of you do-gooders. You smile and say it's okay, and then you get into your car, go home, and sleep in your own bed. You come and go as you please, eat what you want, shower when you want. Your life is yours."

"You know, you had a hard go of it, but can't you be a little friendly?"

"A hard go of it? Precious, I went to jail for fighting over sex."

"What are you talking about? You stabbed your boyfriend in the stomach, didn't you?"

"I was in the kitchen in my condo peeling an apple. That bastard comes in, grabs my tit, and says, 'Can I get some head?' Isn't that romantic? So of course I say no, and then he hits me in the stomach. I fall to my knees; I can't breathe. He, however, doesn't miss a beat. He drops his pants. I still had the knife in my hands, so I used it. At my trial, they said I did it 'cause I found out he was cheating on me. But what do you expect? The government gives medical coverage for Viagra but not birth control. Anyway, then he sues me and I lose everything. So forgive me if I'm not friendly."

"My boyfriend had me give him head while his friends hid so they could watch."

"Men suck, kid."

"Yes, they do." Both women eased up just a little and began a conversation. They talked for a half hour. Megan left to start her assimilation into the program. Liam and Lily went to lunch. During lunch, Lily thanked Liam for the opportunity. Helping Megan seemed not to be all that bad after all.

Daniel was eating lunch while watching ESPN on the wide-screen TV. Death ain't so bad, he thought as the phone rang. "Flowers residence. Daniel speaking."

"You're dead, pal!"

"No kidding! Which angel is this?"

"What the eff does that mean?" the voice growled.

"It means I know I'm dead, so you're a day late and a dollar short."

"Are you nuts?"

"What do you mean?"

"Listen, pal, let's start again. I'm calling to tell you it's coming."

"What's coming?"

"Redemption!" the voice shouted.

"Well, I should hope so. I'd hate to think I went through all this for nothing," Daniel answered calmly.

"What's wrong with you, pal? Are you that used to threatening phone calls?"

"You're human…"

"No ——."

"Who is this?"

"Your worst nightmare!"

"I doubt that. I have some pretty messed-up dreams."

"Don't think I'm joking; I called to tell you you're going down."

"Who is this?"

"I don't like when you mess with my boy," the voice said, angry now.

"I don't know who your boy is, but I'm not a homosexual."

"I'm going to kill you. Do you understand that? Kill you."

"Hey, good luck with that."

"Oh, I get it. You're a New York tough guy. I suppose I'm just a Florida beach bum to you."

The voice screamed something Daniel couldn't make out, and then Daniel said, "Hey, tell me what I'm doing now." Daniel slammed the phone down and finished his lunch.

Lily came home and couldn't wait to tell Daniel about her day. Though at first she had wanted nothing to do with her community service, she told him that after meeting Megan and talking to her, she realized that everyone at some point needed someone. Lily was looking forward to being Megan's big sister. She told Liam how Megan seemed to need her in the same way she needed Daniel. She had never realized how important friendship really was. Daniel heard Lily, but he wasn't listening. The phone call he'd received consumed all of his thoughts.

❖

Heath liked cocaine—a lot. He also liked being thought of as a tough guy. Daniel, he thought, took that away. He had made Heath run away to London. Heath and Brook had had enough of London. They decided to go home. Before leaving, Heath called his coke dealer and told him about Lily and Daniel. The dealer told him to come home and not to worry, saying he'd take care of Daniel. The egocentric dealer called Daniel in order to torment him. He had no idea who he was dealing with. His plan was to slay Daniel and get a big payday. Then he'd be out of the drug dealing business and disappear.

Heath and Brook flew back to Florida on their private jet. During the flight, Heath thought about how his drug dealer would scare the hell out of Daniel—how he would give Daniel a beating. Heath had no idea the terrible cycle he'd set in motion or how Vengeance has a very high price to pay.

❖

The next morning, Lily drove herself to Prodigal Sons & Daughters. She was looking forward to helping Megan.

Megan, however, had her own idea of how Lily could help her. When Lily arrived, Megan met her in the assignment room. These rooms were set up so a parolee and volunteer could meet and talk in private. In the room was a library table and four chairs. The two women sat across from each other.

"So, Megan, how was your first day here?"

"Peachy."

"I was thinking maybe we could get permission and I could take you out shopping."

"Shopping? Is that what I need to fix my life?"

"No, I just figured we could get to know each other."

"Can I ask you something?"

"Of course."

"All that money your family's got—how come you're doing community service?"

"The money my family's got?" Lily said, shocked.

"Oh, Miss Flowers, don't act dumb, I know who you are. In fact, I sat up all night thinking about it. I got an idea—an idea that could save us a lot of time."

"Oh really? What's your idea?"

"Listen up. I don't give a damn about you or your goodwill. But I do care about your bank account. Check this out: We act like best friends, real lovey dovey. I say you're the best; you tell everyone how well I'm doing. As a matter of fact, you decide to donate, oh, let's say a million dollars, to me. You finish this rehab they have you doing, and I get my life back and go on my way."

"I will not do that."

"Okay then, you leave me no choice. I want a new big sister."

"Fine then; let's go."

"You're forgetting something. Liam went through all this trouble. I'm gonna tell him you look down on me and make me feel uncomfortable. Depressed. I don't think you can handle this. I don't know what will happen to me, but you'll end up in jail on the wrong end of a player."

Lily propelled herself across the table. She kicked Megan right in the face, sending blood flying out of her nose, and Megan flew backward in her chair. She slammed onto the floor, Lily on top of her, her fury seething through her pores. She slapped Megan over and over again, screaming the whole time.

Liam and five secretaries burst in when they heard the ruckus. It took all of them to restrain Lily, and then security guards charged in as reinforcements.

"She's crazy! She attacked me! She tried to kill me!" Megan shouted.

"Security, get her out of here!" Liam shouted. The guards escorted Megan from the room, taking her to the infirmary.

Liam threw everyone else out of the room. It was just him and Lily now.

"My God, what happened?"

"Leave me alone. I'm leaving. Do whatever you want to do. Call Judge Amy; tell her I said for her to go hell. We're through. Don't call me; don't talk to me. You wanna help these animals? Go ahead!" Lily slammed the door on Liam on her way out. She hopped into her car and disappeared.

Liam placed Megan under house arrest and started an investigation into what happened. He also called Daniel to tell him Lily was gone again.

"I should kill you," Daniel replied over the phone.

The assignment rooms contained hidden video cameras. The sessions were recorded in case of incidents like this, and to prevent lawsuits. There would be no successful escape plans. Liam watched Megan's blackmail scheme unfold. As far as he was concerned, Megan was going back to jail.

Daniel needed to take a walk after he got off the phone. He took the ferry to the beach. As he walked along the shore, his mind raced. *Where is she this time, and why hasn't she called me? The guy who called—was he after her too? Did he grab her? Is she in danger?*

As Daniel deliberated, he noticed three men approaching him. His reflections interrupted, he stood watching them. *Is this an ambush?* If it was, one of them would break ranks and take the lead. *They have a wolf pack mentality —one alpha, the other two hanging from his balls because they have none of their own.* The men began to close in, one of them stepping in front of the other two. Daniel knew the drill. The one in front would try to distract him; then he'd attack, and the other two would join in. Daniel also knew how to fend off an enemy. He put his hands behind his back and made fists with his fingers, his thumbs sticking straight out. He moved his right shoulder to adjust his weight. The man in the lead made his move. The distraction came in the form of a question.

"Excuse me, sir, where would we rent beach chairs?" asked the man as he pulled out a blackjack.

Before he could even swing his arm, Daniel jammed his thumb into the guy's eye and grabbed his crotch. The would-be attacker dropped the blackjack and doubled over in pain. Daniel scooped up the blackjack and hit him behind the ear. He slammed face-first into the sand, and his two accomplices took off running. Daniel rolled him onto his back. He was out cold, his eye bleeding. A woman who had been sunning herself was startled at the commotion, sat up, and started screaming. Daniel jumped into the ocean and swam over to the pier to hide. Cops and paramedics swarmed the beach. As they put the man on a stretcher, the sunbathing woman pointed toward the pier. The cops talked on their radios, gesturing toward the pier. Daniel swam across the current back to the ferry. He stayed underwater for the most part. Helicopters flew about, and it took him forty-five minutes, but he got back on the ferry without being seen.

When he got back to the penthouse, he took a hot shower. Every muscle in his body ached. He was thankful to be young and strong again. He would have gotten caught in his old body. He lay down and fell asleep, waking an hour later. He got out of bed and walked around the penthouse, calling out for Lily. He got no answer. He sat down in the kitchen, trying to think of where Lily might have gone. The ringing phone brought him back to the moment.

What now? thought Daniel.

❖

Liam sat behind his desk, preparing paperwork. Megan was in lockdown; Liam was sending her back to prison.

Lily walked in. She was sober.

"I'll be home soon, Daniel," she said into her cell phone before she hung up. Lily had a determined look on her face. Liam couldn't recall ever having seen Lily looking this way.

"Lily, before you say anything, I want you to know we recorded your meeting with Megan. I know about the blackmail plot. Don't worry. I'll take care of this."

"Babe, please don't do that."

"Do what, honey?"

"Take care of it. Send Megan back to jail."

"Okay, Lily, listen to me before you do anything crazy."

"Be quiet and listen to me for a second,Liam."

He sat down and stared at her.

"I was going to get drunk when I left. I was about to call Brook when it dawned on me that since I was born, other people have been living my life for me, taking care of my screwups, making sure I never suffered any consequences. Liam, between you and Daniel, I realize I have to live my own life, good or bad. I wanna grow up. I'm twenty-five years old; it's time. I flipped out and attacked Megan. I took my own disappointing life out on her. But I want to help her. Even if I fail, at least I have to try. I owe her at least that much."

"I don't know about this, Lily. If something happens, there could be a lawsuit. We could be shut down. It's a big risk."

"I beat on her and nothing happens to me, but she goes back to jail. Is that justice, Liam?"

"I don't know what you did with Lily, but I like it."

"Does that mean you'll give me another chance?"

"Of course I will. Man, I admire you. I'll have them bring Megan in."

"Thank you, babe."

"No, thank you."

Relieved to know Lily was all right, Daniel could now focus on his next move. First, he needed a gun. The only way was to get them before they got him. He smiled and thought, *Just like the old days.*

With little fanfare, Faith appeared in front of him looking frustrated. She had her arms folded across her chest and was tapping her foot.

"Hey, you!" said Daniel. "Why are you looking at me like that? Is everything all right?"

"You tell me!"

"Well, no actually. Someone wants to kill me. It's just like the old days."

"It's just like the old days 'cause you're acting like you did in the old days."

"Hey, wait a minute; I didn't ask for this!"

"You demanded this."

"What are you talking about?"

"Learn to take responsibility for your actions."

"What did I do?"

"Did you or did you not beat up Heath?"

"So it's Heath."

"You tossed him on the ground. Right in front of his friends. He wants revenge."

"I solved a problem!"

"You don't solve a problem with violence."

"*You* don't, because *you're* an angel."

"Daniel, think about your life as Nicky. Did you have friends besides Chips and the Hump? Was it peaceful living? Did you laugh? Were you carefree?"

"No, of course not."

"That's funny, 'cause that's what life is for."

"Hey, wait a minute; I wasn't the only miserable human being."

"I know that."

"So I'm just like everybody else."

"No, you're dead. Your soul was put into new flesh. You were sent back so you could possibly save yourself."

"I mean when I was Nicky—not now."

"You were like all the other human beings who didn't get it."

"Get what?"

"The universe is like a giant mirror. What you think and what you act upon are a reflection. That reflection manifests as your life. So violence brings about more violence. That's what 'You reap what you sow' means. You're here for salvation, for your own redemption. But you're starting to live for damnation and punishment. So I'll ask you this once: which do you care for? Because you can't have both."

"I want salvation."

"Fill your heart with love, and you can hear your soul sing. It is then that life will unfold before you."

"I don't understand."

133

"Stop acting like a gangster."

"I don't know any other way."

"There's always another way. You just haven't figured it out yet."

"I'll try. Am I really doing that bad?"

"Sit down. I want to tell you a story."

"What kind of story?"

"A Nicky Vocci story. Now sit down." He did as instructed.

"In your past experience, you stole a car. You blew past a stop sign. A police car pulled up behind you with the lights flashing. You sped away, the police chasing you. You ended up doing ninety miles per hour down Avenue V with two police cars behind you and more on their way. Thank goodness is it was 3:30 a.m. and the streets were empty."

Faith paused for a moment. "Suddenly you made a sharp turn onto Knapp Street. You started racing toward the Belt Parkway. You looked in your rearview mirror. You seemed to have lost the police, so you smiled to yourself. That only lasted a second. The lights started flashing again. You pushed down on the pedal, and then you lost control of the car. You bounced off of five parked cars before your car rolled onto its side. You, of course, were unharmed. As you leaped from the debris, you saw house lights coming on. You heard the sirens closing in. You saw Gerritsen Creek before you, so you jumped in and started to swim across. You swam slowly, quietly, and underwater. "

Daniel nodded silently.

"At the same time, a man was having a heart attack," the angel continued. "His wife called 911. The ambulance that was sent couldn't get through because of the car wreckage in the street. The cops tried to clear a path. Firemen showed up to help. The ambulance eventually got through, but it was too late. And in all the excitement, you got away too. Your father gave you a dreadful beating not for what you did, but rather for the attention it brought about. Then he made sure you didn't get caught by the police."

"So I got away with it."

"On the physical plane you did, but not in your soul, where it counts."

"I beat up that guy and swam away. It's the same behavior in a different life."

"Bingo! The universe saw love cry that night. This is your chance to pay back that debt."

"I'll change. I'll make it right."

"I know you will. I gotta go now." Faith vanished, and Daniel attempted something he had never tried before. He dropped to his knees and prayed.

Lily sat across from Megan. They were alone in Liam's office. Megan had a black eye and swollen lip. Lily couldn't believe she was capable of such violence. After sitting in silence for several moments, Megan spoke.

"If you're here to apologize, don't. However, if you wanna go again, let's go."

"Megan, I'm here to beg for your forgiveness."

"Sorry, kid. I don't have that in me. But don't worry about it. Hell, my boyfriend beat me a lot worse. He never marked my face though. You know, that way there's no evidence."

"Oh, Megan, I'm so sorry."

"What do you want?"

"I want to help you."

"Oh, you do? I got confused when you kicked me in the face."

"I can't believe I did that. You have no idea how sorry I am."

"No, Lily, I don't. How sorry are you?"

"For one thing, I made sure you're not going back to jail. I promise I'll keep you here, and if you'd like, I'll take you shopping for a new wardrobe."

"A new wardrobe?"

"Megan, we can go shopping. Two girls chatting and getting to know each other—it might be fun. Plus I know a lot of people. I'll help you find work if you want."

"Oh, what the hell ... Okay, Lily, you got it. I guess I deserved a beating for what I did."

"No, you didn't. And I'd like to make it up to you."

"When are we going?"

"I'll pick you up tomorrow. Let's say ten a.m."

"It's a date!"

"Thank you, Megan."

"No, Lily. Thank you." Lily felt a sense of purpose.

Megan was taken back to her room. She was told the next day she'd be taken back in population. She took a hot bath, and the water pruned her skin as she recited the Lord's Prayer. Razor in hand, Megan found it easier to succumb to suicidal thoughts than to resist them. The tub water turned red, and Megan was gone.

❖

At 6:30 p.m. Liam hung up the phone in his office. Journalists were at the front gate. Police investigators scoured every inch of Prodigal Sons & Daughters. Prison investigators still had their investigations to do.

❖

Lily was waiting to go out to dinner. Liam hadn't told her yet. When Daniel opened the terrace door for Liam, Lily had her back to him, looking out over the Intracoastal.

Without turning around, Lily said, "Well, you showed up. Late. No phone call. Guess what, Tiger? No phone call, no date, so you might as well turn around—"

"Lily, Megan's dead. She killed herself."

Lily spun around in shock. *"What?"*

"I'm sorry, Lily. You were just going to keep talking, so I figured I'd just say it."

"Liam..." Lily went numb. In one moment, her life was never going to be the same. She was in the world between dreams and reality, where one's mind experiences the nightmare of dealing with the pain coming from the heart. The mind says, "It's all right," but the heart knows better. As the pressure builds right before the explosion, tears burst from the eyes. Liam took Lily into his arms. She deflated; the only physical strength was her crying. Her sobs came from deep within her core. There were no comforting words. Lily latched onto Liam as if he was a life preserver and she was drowning.

Daniel could see the two of them out on the terrace. As Lily embraced Liam, he wished he could be Liam. But then he reminded himself that he was there to help. For right now, he would let them be. The embrace ended with Lily laughing and wiping her eyes.

"Sorry, Liam, I get crazy."

"Lily, that's not crazy. You're hurt and you showed it."

"I don't do vulnerable."

"Lily, that was beautiful, it—"

"Yeah, okay. I'm gonna lie down, so could you leave?"

"Lily, wait, where are you going?" Lily left Liam standing alone on the terrace. She walked down the hall and into her room, and there she lay down on the bed, her mind racing. *See what happens when you try to help? People suck.* Then she got up and walked to the wet bar. Lily didn't do emotions. Not sober, anyway.

Daniel walked onto the terrace. Liam had his back turned to him.

"Yo! Sorry about Megan!"

"Thanks. Hey, how come she's so callous? I mean, what's so hard about her life?"

"Me, I'm poor. So I bitch and moan, and people say, 'Yeah, it's tough.' But now I'm rich, and suddenly I got no reason to bitch and moan, 'cause I got cash and I got stuff. Liam, people don't get that you can fill up on the outside and be empty on the inside. I'm poor, and I bitch because life's tough without money. Lily says, 'Why am I not happy? I got it all; I got money.'"

"She's selfish and cold. I'm about to lose everything. Lily Flowers is upset. You know what? I'm a fool. I'm running around trying to save the world. For what? Some demented soul kills herself, and now they're coming after me? I'm done!"

"Liam, you're never gonna be done. You have a good heart. No matter what happens, you'll always be helping people."

"Don't act like you know me, 'cause you don't."

"I admire you."

"Then you're a bigger fool than I thought."

"Yo! Turn around and look at me." Liam turned around. He had been crying. He wiped his eyes and rushed past Daniel, heading for the elevator. Then he saw Lily drinking. He turned and headed toward the wet bar.

"So that's what your answer is? Getting drunk?"

"Saint Crazy, get your ass out of here or I'll tell Daniel to throw you off the terrace."

"You're not chasing me away. We need to talk."

"Talk about what? Did Megan come back to life? That's two resurrections I missed."

Liam stormed away. As he got on the elevator, Lily called out in a loud Southern drawl, "Don't come back, y'all."

Lily made herself a pitcher of screwdriver. She took off her clothes and walked naked to the hot tub, passing Daniel on the terrace. Daniel watched the beauty sway past him. He walked off as if he didn't notice her.

He took an ice-cold shower. That didn't help, so he took matters into his own hands. Of course, that was the moment Faith appeared. Daniel pulled the bed covers up over his lap, mortified.

"So, what's up?" Faith asked, smiling.

"What do you want?"

"Did I come at the wrong time? Obviously your hands are full."

"Could you turn around for a second?"

"Is it because my gown is sheer? You want to see my butt?"

"What?"

"I'm just trying to help."

"I need to put my pants on."

"It's not a sin to please yourself. Unless, of course, you try to shake someone's hand right afterward."

"What?"

"Oh, come on, that's funny."

"I am not having this conversation with you!"

"Why not? I mean, you can hold your own."

"Enough! You're enjoying this way too much." Daniel stood up naked in front of Faith and spread out his arms. "I'm not getting dressed." He started to spin around slowly. "Do you like what you see? 'Cause now I'm naked."

"It's a nice suit. Now, could you stop turning so we can talk?" Daniel stopped and put his hands on his hips, glaring at Faith, who began laughing.

"You're so serious. Like I care that you're naked."

"What do you want? I know Lily and Liam are fighting again. I know somehow I have to put them together. I know they'd be better off apart. So what do you want?"

"First of all, they love each other, and love will find a way. They fight because of Insecurity. You're here to help yourself by helping them. You tend to forget that. Now, what I want is for you to go stop Liam before he hurts Heath."

"What? Liam's a sweetheart; he won't hurt Heath. Besides, what does that a-hole have to do with this?"

"Liam's hurt. He's going to find out Heath hired that drug dealer to hurt you. You know, the violence that you started. Well, then Liam's gonna go beat up Heath. If he does, he'll accidentally kill him—an unexpected misfortune that will destroy his life. Lily will drink, do drugs, go from man to man, and finally overdose. The world will lose two more, and the universe will cry, and you'll wind up a slave in Pride's realm."

"What about you?"

"Me? I'll be fine. Hey, you're naked."

"What kind of angel are you? You're like a wise-ass pervert."

"Daniel, you gotta learn how to relax and have fun."

"Relax! You do remember I died, right? And that I've been caught up in your craziness ever since?"

"You never learned how to live," Faith said as she shook her head. "Humans. You can please yourselves, so you make it a sin. You make the human body evil with the help of lust. You don't appreciate the beauty that is death. So how can you celebrate life? Humans go to sleep not knowing if they'll come back, but yet they wake up every morning like they deserve it instead of realizing the gift they've been given."

"I never thought of it like that."

"Daniel, you have another gift. It's called laughter. Use it."

"I'll try."

"Get dressed and go stop Liam. He's at Prodigal Sons &Daughters. Oh, and Lily's sleeping naked on a lounge chair if you want another peek."

"No thanks."

And just like that, Faith was gone. Daniel got dressed and started out to get Liam. But first he ran out to the terrace for a quick peek.

Daniel hopped into the Bentley. As he raced toward Prodigal Sons & Daughters, Faith appeared. "I was kidding about the peek."

Daniel laughed. "You're crazy; I love it."

"Update. Pride just grabbed that drug dealer's soul. He was shot to death about an hour ago."

"Who shot him?"

"Another gang member. He failed to kill you. Got two gang members beaten up and arrested, and brought about a police investigation."

"This is my fault. I started all this by beating up Heath."

"Yes, Daniel, that's right. Every soul on Earth is a link in a great chain."

"So every action sets off a reaction for good or bad."

"Exactly. That's why you're saving your soul by saving Lily's and Liam's."

"From this moment on, I'll try to change for the better."

"I'm proud of you. Start by stopping Liam. Good luck."

Daniel pulled into Prodigal Sons & Daughters. As he parked

the Bentley, Liam came out of his office and headed toward his car. Daniel called out to him.

"Liam, where are you going in such a hurry?"

"I'm going over to Heath's house. I'm going to beat the crap out of him. Then I'm going to sleep with his sister."

"And what will that prove?"

"Look, Daniel, I don't know why you're here, but you won't believe what I just found out."

"That Heath hired a drug dealer to beat the crap out of me."

"No, Daniel, to kill you. He was hired to kill you."

"I know all about it, Liam. They already tried; they didn't do so well."

"I just heard from the drug dealer's girlfriend that he's now dead and it's Heath's fault, so it's time for him to pay."

"You're frustrated with Lily, and you're gonna take it out on Heath. If you do this, you're no better than him."

"Well, Daniel, tell me—what should I do?"

"Go make up with Lily."

"Lily... All I want to do is love her, and all she does is push me away."

"Don't tell me; tell Lily."

"Why do you care?"

"You're a good man, Liam. Don't be like me. You don't want a life of violence. You don't have the temperament for it. Anyone can hurt and destroy. The brave help and put others first. Go fall in love. Live life."

"I won't go to Heath's, but I won't go over to Lily's either."

Liam got into his car. Daniel tried to talk to him, but Liam ignored him and sped off. Daniel stood in the parking lot, looked up at the sky, and yelled, "Now what?"

Lily awoke to a hangover. She raced into her room, wondering if Daniel had seen her naked. She got her sweats on and staggered out to the kitchen. She made herself a cup of tea. Reeling, she took her tea to bed. As she lay there, she remembered throwing Liam out. She felt bad about that. She thought she would like to love him, but she felt they were different people and it wouldn't work out.

She did like having him around, as she found him very sweet. She rolled onto her side and thought, *Who would be stupid enough to fall in love with a stupid bitch like me?*

Daniel sat in his car and suddenly had a recollection. He remembered Brooklyn Bob. He had been a second father to Daniel when he was Nicky Vocci. He taught the boys how to survive on the streets. Brooklyn Bob was six feet six inches tall and had rugged good looks. He called Brooklyn his borough and acted as if he owned it. The Hump's father gave him the name. Brooklyn Bob was also Irish. He taught Knick Knack, Chips, and the Hump how to be deliberate with every move. Brooklyn Bob calculated his whole life. He used to say, "It ain't illegal if you don't get caught" and "forget 'em if they can't take a joke."

Most of all, Brooklyn Bob was a treacherous assassin. He hated what he referred to as noise. If you were noise to Bob, he made sure you were silenced. Nicky loved Brooklyn Bob. He wanted to be just like him.

Sitting in the car, Daniel realized his whole life as Nicky Vocci was wrong. He became confused. How could annihilation of anything good be a way of life? Awareness came upon him. This was a chance to make it right. He already knew what he had been brought back for, but now he could feel it.

Repentance. He honestly wanted to change his conduct. He must do whatever it takes to save his soul. He must get Liam and Lily together.

Liam sat on the jetty. *How many times must I be shit on? How much loss is enough?* He was fortunate in life. All he wanted was to give back and help people make the world a better place. He loved Lily. He always had. He wanted to spend his life with her. They both wound up apart and in many bad relationships. Life was always saying no to him.

Liam sat there, dismal and discouraged. He began to cry.

TO SAVE A SOUL: PART 4

T he next morning, Daniel was making eggs for Lily when Faith appeared.

"Truth needs to show you something!"

Abruptly, Daniel found himself sitting next to Truth. He was back in the auditorium.

Liam stepped off the penthouse elevator.

"Lily?" he called out.

Lily appeared from her room. With her hair wrapped in a towel, she was wearing a terry cloth robe. Liam spoke deeply from the bottom of his heart.

"Lily, I know how afraid you get, and how you think we're different people. Push me away, curse me, but Lily, I love you. I always have. I could spend the rest of my life making you happy. I will be the best man I can. Please just give us a chance."

Lily became enchanted by Liam. Her whole essence filled with love. It stuck in her throat. She did not speak. A smile spread across her face as she opened her arms. The two embraced. Lily was soft and warm. The towel on her head dropped to the floor. The aroma of strawberries and vanilla pervaded Liam's nostrils.

Lily stepped back and dropped her robe. She tore off Liam's shirt. As Lily rubbed Liam's powerful chest, Liam pulled Lily's voluptuous body onto his. The two fell to the floor and began to caress and make love.

"I know you guys are in charge," Daniel said to Faith, "but on Earth that was rude. I mean, you just come along and rip me out of my body. Now Lily's probably worried about me, and she's probably hungry too, 'cause I was making breakfast."

Truth responded, "First of all, that's not your body. We made it. We lent it to you. Second, we know what we're doing. Third, I doubt Lily's thinking about you or breakfast right now."

"Her mouth is full by now anyway," said Faith.

Truth giggled. "Faith, you're so bad!"

"What's going on?" Daniel asked confusedly.

"It's working. Liam and Lily are making love. I didn't think you would want to be there. Besides, Truth has a moment of your past."

Daniel turned to Truth. "A moment of my past?"

"Yes, Daniel, we have to go over something."

"It's gonna be okay, sweetie," said Faith.

"Oh, stop babying him, Faith."

Daniel laughed. "She has her mouth full. Very funny."

"Oh, come on; it was funny."

"Faith, Daniel, we have work to do."

"What work?" said Daniel. "They're doing the horizontal bop. What more do you want?"

"Don't emphasize love as sex," Faith replied.

"What do you mean?"

"Love is much more."

"I know that. Sex is the fun part."

Truth and Faith both laughed.

"Now what's so funny?" Daniel asked.

Truth replied, "We want them to have a relationship. Love that's mental, physical, and spiritual. It's the only journey worth taking with another."

"Give him a break," said Faith. "He's only human; he doesn't understand."

"We have to teach him."

"I'm sitting in between you two, and you talk like I'm not here," said Daniel.

"Yes, Daniel, sorry about that," said Truth. "Now back to the task at hand. You have the power to call up the past. This power could help you grow and heal. You got confused about your memory of Brooklyn Bob. Do you know what you are confused about?"

"I guess the way Nicky was—or how I was as Nicky. It was ... I don't know ... okay to be cruel. Why would I find that all right, Truth?"

"Daniel, I think your soul is healing. If that's so, it means our experiment is working and you will get better. Pride will lose his hold on you."

"That means anyone can be saved," said Faith. "Oh, Daniel! Oh, Truth! How wonderful would that be... humans loving and caring for one another?"

149

"That would be great," said Truth, "but let's do one soul at a time."

"Yeah, I'm first!" Daniel interjected.

"And let's be unselfish too," Daniel said as he gave Truth a fierce stare. Truth just smiled at him. Truth explained that they were going to witness a moment with Brooklyn Bob. This was a conversation that took place in Bob's car two weeks after Nicky killed Lisa. The lights went down and the projector came on.

Brooklyn Bob looked powerful as he sat next to Nicky. To Daniel it was like a movie. There was no sentiment attached to the image.

"Your head on right, boy?" Brooklyn Bob asked. "Don't lie to me. I saw her. She was a pretty kid."

"Yeah ...what a shame. It is what it is, right?"

"She had some set. I remember thinking to myself, 'Look at the size of those fun bags! Nicky is a lucky little prick.'"

Nicky laughed. "Yeah, I'm gonna miss them, Brooklyn Bob."

"Guys like us have no business falling in love. We're hoodlums, not husbands."

"Dad got married."

"And he got sloppy and that prick cop killed him. You lost a father. Your mom lost her husband. I ain't leaving a widow. Kids take up too much time. When I go, who will care?"

"I will, and so will Chips and the Hump."

"Thanks, kid. I'm just saying don't fall in love. To me, broads are giant receptacles. Love can make you slow and stupid. Worrying about a family can get you dead. You're a great hood. You're gonna have a lot more money and power your way."

"You're right. I don't need to go through this stuff again. I got enough to worry about."

"Now you're talking, kid. Let's go get the money from these two fools."

"Your money or your life!"

The image faded with the two men snickering.

Truth spoke. "You took another life that day. Faith gave up. You lost faith, and your destiny was sealed."

"Or so we thought," Faith said.

"I know I caused a lot of damage. But I can feel it; I want to make amends."

"Sweetie, can you feel your attitude change? Your soul is healing."

"I can't make up for yesterday's mistakes, can I?"

"Remember, Daniel: yesterday's experience gains wisdom, and attainment makes for a better today," Truth said.

"What?"

Faith responded. "Lily and Liam have the physical part. Now is your time to help them learn the spiritual and mental aspects."

"I want the woman I love to be happy," Daniel said.

Truth smiled. "Nice, Daniel. Nice."

Daniel found himself sitting in the Bentley, which was parked at the beach. He got out of the car, stripped to his boxers, and went for a swim.

❖

151

Liam rolled off Lily covered in sweat, exhausted, and happy. Resting on Liam's chest, Lily closed her eyes and began to nap. Liam felt so lucky. He was astonished by Lily's extraordinary figure. A smile crossed his lips. Both nestled together.

Insecurity watched Liam and Lily sleep. He smiled to himself and thought, *Go ahead and get really close; I'll just sit back and wait.* He whispered in Lily's ear, "You're mine, bitch." Then he vanished.

Daniel was smiling as he approached the Bentley. Faith sat on the hood, holding a towel.

"Insecurity snuck up on Lily and Liam. They were napping."

"They were napping? Never mind. What happened?"

"He did nothing. He didn't plant suggestive seeds. Just watched them sleep."

"I did it! He gave up, right? That's why he didn't do anything."

"Combative angels never give up. Their whole existence is based on trying to tempt human beings. Pride, Fear, Anger, Lust, Suspicion, Insecurity—they crop up anytime; that's all they do."

"So I am there when they do?"

"That's all this is about."

"I wanna help; I really do."

"And you will. Get over to Lily's. I'll see you later."

❖

Daniel arrived at the penthouse. Lily was alone on the terrace. Lily told him that she had slept with Liam, and then she said, "Liam wants us to move in together."

"Good news, right?"

"Daniel, we went on a date. He was helping me with parole. So, of course, I go trolling for penis. Spread those legs, girl!"

"What the hell is wrong with you?"

"What's wrong is we're rushing along. We'll play house then break up. That's what always happens."

"Lily, stop it; you two are in love. That won't happen".

"I don't know if I love him. I know I'm a selfish bitch. I don't think I'm ready for commitment. I mean… devotion is not one of my strong points."

"You're right. You'll just drift from man to man. Then you'll get old, lose your looks, and die alone. Don't change, 'cause the drinking is working out great."

"Daniel! How dare you!"

"Sorry, Lily, but I'm a nuts-and-bolts guy. I call it as I see it."

Daniel and Lily sat down. Lily told Daniel she always wanted love. She was tired of being alone, but she didn't know how to have a relationship. Most people annoyed her.

Daniel laughed and said he felt the same way though he was getting older and was alone. He then said, "Lily, like me, you keep pushing people away, but there will come a time when there's no one left to push."

They talked for over an hour. Afterward, Lily packed an overnight bag. Daniel drove her over to Liam's igloo. She agreed to give it a shot. As Daniel drove away, he saw Insecurity appear and disappear, and he stopped the car.

"Is everything all right?" Lily yelled out quizzically. Daniel stepped out of the car and waved. He got back in, and as he drove off, he thought, *Don't look in the rearview mirror.*

❖

Donald stood on the stool crying. The rope around his neck itched.

Insecurity whispered in his ear, "Jump."

Donald saw his body swinging, and an ungodly dwarf stood before him.

"Who are you?" Donald asked.

"I am the soul collector!"

Donald felt a chill as the dark shadow of Pride engulfed him, and he was gone. Insecurity was victorious again.

❖

Lily called the Pink Parrot and ordered delivery: salmon steak, wild rice, and steamed asparagus. She set the table and lit candles. Liam came home and sat at the dinner table. He looked despondent and miserable and was not eating. Lily got up and walked over and sat on Liam's lap.

"Don't ignore me. Talk to me."

Liam told Lily that not only could lawsuits from this could ruin him, but he could be charged with criminal negligence as well. Bankruptcy was one thing, but jail was something he didn't know if he could do.

Lily cradled Liam's face and kissed him gently on the lips. "You gotta eat, babe." She stayed on his lap and fed him. After Liam finished eating, they stripped and went for a swim. They made love in the ocean. The moonlight danced on the ocean. The two lovers went back into the house. They showered and then made love again. Lily lay down on the bed wrapped in a towel. Liam massaged Lily's feet and legs with a moisturizer. Lily groaned with pleasure and she heard herself saying to Liam, "Oh God, I love you."

Liam leaned over and kissed her. He smiled and said nothing. Then he wiped the lotion from his hands. He lay down and turned on the TV. Lily rolled on top of him. The two lay like that watching Dancing with the Stars. Love grew stronger, and sleep crept in.

The following morning, the phone was ringing off the hook. Liam's lawyer told him to come to Prodigal Sons & Daughters. Upon arriving, Liam and Lily received a hero's welcome. It seemed old clients had assembled to support Liam. Thanks to Liam Patrick and Prodigal Sons & Daughters, these women were off parole. They had been able to turn their lives around.

Megan's family knew the situation. Even they praised Prodigal Sons and Daughters. Thanks to e-mails, letters, and phone calls, the lead investigator made a proclamation of innocence. Lily was so happy; she called Daniel. After telling him the news, she asked him to pick up hamburgers, chicken, hot dogs, and a keg of beer. Liam and Lily had a giant celebratory barbecue. Over 150 people showed up and a good time was had by all. Lily witnessed the miracle of people helping each other.

Liam was a hopeless romantic, and romance made his life worth living. O'Keefe was Lily's favorite artist. Her work was on exhibition at the Norton Museum, and Liam got tickets and planned quite the day.

At the museum, the couple came to rest at the depiction of a Mexican chapel. They sat fixated on the painting. Lily clasped Liam's hand and rested her head on his shoulder. At that moment, the world could have ended as far as Liam was concerned. Once in a while, life gives you a perfect moment. This was one of those.

By noon, they had finished seeing the entire exhibit. Lily was hungry, and Liam had rented the museum's private garden. Two dozen roses waited for her along with a catered picnic lunch of fried chicken, potato salad, and corn on the cob.

After lunch, the two went to Palm Beach International Airport. They boarded Liam's jet and flew to New York City, where Liam took Lily shopping. They got back to the Igloo around 9:00 p.m., went skinny-dipping in the ocean, and made love for hours. They finally fell asleep, their behinds touching —or cheek-to-cheek, if you prefer.

Daniel called while they were eating breakfast the following morning. Judge Amy wanted to see Lily that afternoon. Liam told Daniel he'd take Lily over. Right after his call with Daniel, Sister Helen called. She was a nun at the orphanage Liam had built. God's Own was home to many abandoned children. Helen asked Liam to please stop by. Liam asked Lily if they could stop there first on the way to court.

Lily said of course. She couldn't believe somebody could be so good. Liam, however, thought it was no big deal.

LOVE IS ABSOLUTELY INVINCIBLE

God's Own orphanage was located in Boynton Beach. It was a run-down motel that Liam owned. Four years earlier, Liam had found a nun sitting in his office. There was a mystique about her—a kind of powerful spiritualism. Liam couldn't put his finger on it. Whatever it was, the sixty-something nun captivated Liam.

Her name was Sister Helen. She told Liam she admired him but would like to help people before they got in trouble. They went for breakfast. At breakfast, Sister Helen told Liam her idea. She wanted to find homes for abandoned children. She would take only six at a time. Their ages could range from six months to six years. Liam laughed at the six six six. Sister Helen assured Liam that the last thing Satan wanted to do was mess with her. By the time they left the diner, Liam was sold, and so God's Own was born, and it had been placing children ever since. Sister Helen said the children came in lost and then found love and were lost no more.

Lily looked at Liam after he finished telling her the story of the orphanage.

"You're my rock star and angel," Lily said.

"No, Sister Helen is. I just provided a place and some cash."

They sped along the A1A, heading to God's Own. Lily massaged the back of Liam's neck. Once again, Lily sent Liam to paradise. A mile or so farther along, Judge Amy called Liam.

"Hello ... Yes, I know, your honor. Okay, I'll be sure to tell her." Liam hung up.

"Tell me what?"

"The judge found another woman for you to help."

"F—— that! Excuse my French."

"Lily, this is your parole. We're trying to keep you out of jail."

"Honey, I'm going to be very frank. I can't and won't help another psycho."

They pulled into God's Own and parked. An argument started. Lily refused to help anyone else—or even try to. Liam tried to convince her. His pleading did nothing for Lily.

"I got drunk, killed my dog, and crashed my car. I'm sorry about that, but I can't deal with another suicide. I can't take this. Liam, I think I love you; don't push this."

"Can we talk about this later?"

"Are you listening? There's nothing to talk about."

Liam got out of the car and walked around to open Lily's door. She got out, and after glancing at Liam, she walked conspicuously ahead of him. As she marched along, Sister Helen appeared at the front door. Lily stopped in her tracks, appearing to be in awe.

"Come in, dear," Sister Helen said, "but leave that attitude outside."

Lily stood there for a second. Liam caught up to her, and Lily grabbed his hand. The two walked together into God's Own.

Liam had spent a million dollars on the orphanage. It was the best facility of its kind, boasting both a playground and an indoor pool. Sister Helen and her staff nurtured the children and made sure they were placed in good homes.

It was apparently time to go over the budget. While Liam and Sister Helen went over expenditures and income, a bored Lily took a walk. About an hour later, Sister Helen's aide rushed in.

"Sister Helen, come with me. You have to see this!"

Liam, Sister Helen, and the aide hurried to the playground. There sat Lily, talking with four-year-old Emily F.

Sister Helen smiled at this sight. "Oh God, it's a miracle," she said.

Emily F. had been found abandoned on a church altar when only six months old. She was given to Sister Helen and was the first orphan at God's Own. Emily F. was seemingly normal in every way. She had wavy blond hair and blue eyes. An all-American girl, she looked as if she could be on a box of Wheaties. But in four years, Emily F. had never uttered a word. No doctor could figure out why. But now she was sitting on a bench having a conversation with Lily Flowers. She was giggling and happy. Lily and Emily were enjoying a moment of hilarity.

Sister Helen asked Liam if Lily was still on parole. Liam told her that Megan was the woman Lily had tried to help.

"Why am I not surprised?" Sister Helen said. Then she went into her office and called Judge Amy. Lily had a gift with children, and Sister Helen was going to use it.

❖

By the time Liam and Lily left God's Own, Lily was the new caregiver.

Liam dropped Lily off at the penthouse. He had to be in New York in the morning, and Lily wanted to prepare for her first day.

Daniel drew a bath. As Lily bathed, Daniel cooked tuna steaks, wild rice, and steamed carrots. Lily asked Daniel to have dinner with her. Lily knew whose advice she'd take.

"So you're gonna take care of orphans?"

"That's right. Judge Amy okayed it. Of course, I don't think Sister Helen takes no for an answer. So starting tomorrow, I'm the new caregiver for the nursery."

"Hmm. Wow, that's interesting."

"What's that supposed to mean?"

"You go to trial for DWI. You get parole and your license suspended for life. You have to do a year of community service or three years in prison. Correct?"

"Something like that."

"Liam agrees to help you."

"You know all this; what's your point?"

"The woman you were doing community service with offs herself, so Liam introduces you to an orphanage-running nun. And now you're gonna be a nanny. Is that right, or am I way off base?"

"That's right. So?"

"That, Lily, my friend, is interesting."

"I guess."

"Anything else pressing on your mind?"

"I think I love Liam."

"That's great. I told you to just give it a chance."

"I'm in love, I think. Oh, Daniel, what's wrong with me?"

"You're like me, Lily, selfish and self-absorbed. You think, 'If I love him, what's in it for me?' Or 'Why does he act like that; what does he want from me?'"

"I guess."

"You guess?"

"Daniel, I don't know. I'm always miserable and confused. I'm nuts. Why would anyone want to love me? What do I want out of a relationship?"

"You know, Lily, I was always miserable until I found out."

"Found out what?"

"Life is not taking; it's giving."

"What's that supposed to mean?"

"In other words, find out what you can bring to Liam. Forget what you can get from him."

"How do I do that?"

"Stop putting Lily first. Try to put others first."

"What are you, Gandhi or something?"

"I'm done. I tried."

"Wait, Daniel. I'll try; I just don't know how."

"Do you wanna know what I've been doing—what makes me want to be selfless?"

"Your love for me?"

"It's all about you, Lily."

"I'm kidding. You do love me, right?"

"Yes, Lily, I love and care about you."

"Thanks, Daniel. I love and care for you too. I can talk to you; you listen to me."

"So does Liam."

"Yeah, he does too."

"So what's the matter, Lily?"

"I really believe I'm too selfish for love, and I don't know what to do. Liam scares me. What if he gets tired of me? I'm such a high-maintenance bitch! I don't know how else to act."

"Lily, stop it now! You wanna know what I've been doing? I've been praying."

"What?"

"You heard me. I've been praying."

"To God?"

"Who else do you pray to?"

"Oh, Daniel, let's not go there."

"Are you afraid of God?"

"No, but maybe I'm a little afraid of you. Daniel, you're like this big tough guy. You're not afraid of anything, and now you tell me you pray. I can get this fluff from Liam."

"Why don't you shut up and give something new a try?"

"Don't you dare talk to me that way!"

"I'm sorry, but sometimes you're so frustrating."

"So get out!"

"Lily, I—"

"Get out!" Lily screamed.

Daniel left the table and went to his room. As Daniel packed, Lily sat on the terrace and began to cry. Suddenly she got up and went to her room, where she knelt by the end of her bed.

"God, it's me, Lily. If you're there, help..."

When she finished, she turned and saw Daniel standing in the doorway. Daniel was holding his suitcase. Lily walked over and hugged him. Lily and Daniel watched TV for the rest of the evening and then said good night.

The next morning, Daniel pulled the Bentley into God's Own. He opened the car door for Lily. As Lily went inside, Sister Helen emerged. She scrutinized Daniel's every move.

"You're not whom you appear to be."

"I'm sorry, Sister?"

"You have the physique of a healthy young man, but your eyes are old and tired. Who are you?"

"I'm Lily's houseman."

Just then Faith appeared. "You walk with Faith, I see," said Sister Helen.

"You can see her?"

"God bless you, young man." Sister Helen turned and walked away.

Daniel stood there with his mouth open, motionless.

"Are you okay?" Faith asked.

"She saw you. That nun can see angels."

"All human beings can see angels."

"Then how come Lily and Liam can't see you? As a matter of fact, no one can see you — except that nun."

"You can't see us with your eyes. You see angels with your heart. Angels are that guarded utterance in your ear, that pleasant sensation, a flutter that tells you everything is all right. Most humans disregard us. Humans depend on eyesight instead of insight. Sister Helen gets it. Lily's in the right place."

"I thought I was supposed to save Lily."

"It takes more than just one person. Between you, Liam, Sister Helen, and us angels, Lily's gonna be all right. But remember, Daniel, she would have killed herself in New York. You saved her; therefore, we all get to help her. One soul helping another—Love's great plan."

"So I'm finished?"

"You tell me." Daniel took a moment and then said, "No, not yet. And I don't know why. But it's not done; there's something else."

"Remember: combative angels never give up."

"I will."

"Keep Lily on this path. It may not be easy."

"Nothing about Lily is or ever has been easy." Faith kissed Daniel's cheek and then vanished. Daniel got back in the Bentley, drove to Deerfield Beach, and went for a swim.

Months turned into years. Lily kept praying. Sister Helen taught her to meditate. Slowly Lily's attitude changed, and her life followed suit. She found a mentor in Sister Helen. Daniel became like an older brother to her. Lily began to trust her heart. Her relationship with Liam grew strong. She forgave herself for past transgressions and started to become aware of herself. She found she could enjoy intimacy. She loved when Liam touched her. Who cared about all those other men? She really never enjoyed that kind of sex. It was more or less the attention she had craved. Liam loved her unconditionally. She didn't have to please people anymore. Liam and Lily were like two peas in a pod.

Liam, being an old soul, was earnest. He held deep thoughts and was always fussing about something. Then he started to pray with Lily. He started to feel the joy of giving— not out of guilt or obligation, but rather because of how light and free his heart became. Liam also learned flexibility. And ultimately, Liam learned how to laugh at himself.

Lily started to believe that life is not about wants and needs but is rather about being trustworthy and reliable, and having integrity. She became less selfish and wanted to give rather than take. She too became lighthearted and free. Daniel joked that together Lily and Liam made one normal person.

Lily's drive came from the children. She stayed on at God's Own well after she completed her parole. She loved being surrounded by children: McKenna, Riley, Jack, Kadyn, Shane, Ann, Edward, Liz, James, and, of course, Emily F. Lily loved them more than herself—actually, more than life itself. It was that love that ultimately saved her. She finally knew how to love and be loved.

Then came Valentine's Day and Liam's marriage proposal. Liam's love for Lily was so straightforward and genuine that it took Lily's breath away. No one had ever come close to loving her like that. Lily said yes, and after dinner, the two of them made love all night. The next day they asked Sister Helen to help them adopt Emily F., before they even picked a wedding date. Lily and Liam's parents rented a Boca Raton resort for an engagement party. It was going to be a who's who of wealthy families, which meant a media circus. Lily's father flew in from Europe. Liam's parents came down from New York. Two powerful families were forming an alliance, and the world wanted to participate.

The morning of the party, Sister Helen called Daniel, who was at the beach. She said Lily didn't sound good and asked if Daniel would check on her. Daniel said he would and said good-bye. He went back to his swim. He had made dinner for Lily and Liam the night before, and everything had been fine then. Daniel saw no emergency.

Liam was working in Miami. He tried several times to reach Lily. He called Daniel to find out what was going on. As Daniel was leaving the beach, he told Liam he'd call him back. Liam told Daniel to have Lily call him.

Daniel stepped off the elevator into the penthouse.

"Lily! You home? Yo, kid, you here?"

Much to Daniel's horror, there was Lily. She was facedown on the bed. A half-empty bottle of vodka was on the nightstand, and an empty bottle of sleeping pills lay on the floor.

"Lily, noooo!"

He turned her over and put his ear to her chest. As he listened for a heartbeat, he heard giggling. He sat up. There, squatting in the corner was Insecurity.

Daniel jumped to his feet. "You can't have her!"

By the time Insecurity stood, Daniel had his hands around his throat, squeezing his larynx. The combative angel dug his talons into Daniel's arms, and a savage fight began. Daniel was in control. Insecurity was getting weak when the awareness came upon Daniel that there was a better way. He released Insecurity and said, "Do you want to go home?"

"You're that soul! The one called Nicky Vocci! Pride needs you. You can't say no to Pride; come with me."

"I found love, or love found me. I don't need Pride anymore. Take my hand, and I'll show you. You don't have to do this. You can be better; we all can. Trust me."

Daniel knelt down and opened his arms. "Give love a chance. You come with me."

"What do you know about love?"

"Nothing, but if you look for forgiveness, you usually find love too. Faith saved me, and she can save you too. Please let us help you."

Just then Lily called out, "Daniel, be quiet; I'm tryin' to sleep."

Insecurity looked at Daniel in disbelief.

"That's the power of love, brother," Daniel said.

With that, Insecurity took Daniel's hand. "I want to go home. Will you take me?"

"I'd like nothing more," Daniel said.

"Daniel, I need more sleep," said Lily. "Wake me in an hour. I'll have plenty of time to get ready."

"Sorry, Lily. Go back to sleep."

Faith was in the living room, waiting for Daniel. She couldn't believe it when he and Insecurity walked in side by side.

"He wants to go home," Daniel said.

Faith said, "We have to hide him. This means war; Pride is not gonna be pleased. You don't want to deal with hurt pride."

"Oh blah, blah, blah. We got this," Daniel said.

Truth and the other angels came and took Insecurity home.

Daniel didn't miss a beat. He looked at Faith and asked, "What just happened? I thought Lily was dead."

"We didn't take her, because of you. It turns out we were right. She'll be fine. She'll wake up and won't remember a thing. And now we know that maybe we can save the combative angels. We never thought that they might want to come back. Thank you, Daniel. This experiment exceeded any expectations. But there's also work yet to be done."

"Like what?"

"Call Liam. Tell him Lily's fine and just wants to sleep in." "Liam! I forgot."

"Go ahead. I'll see you later."

That night, Lily looked exquisite as she emerged from the Bentley. Liam parked at the service entrance to avoid the reporters out front. Lily stood face-to-face with Daniel. The two embraced.

Daniel heard Lisa's voice in his ear: "Nicky, I forgive you. I'll always love you. Now I set you free. We both have a second chance, babe. Let's make the most of it. Good-bye." Then the voice was gone. Daniel thought it was a hallucination.

"Well, Daniel, how do I look?" Lily asked.

"Fabulous, like a dream."

"You're so sweet."

"Liam's waiting!"

"Good. I'm worth it."

The two of them laughed.

"Get going, silly girl," said Daniel. Lily walked toward the door and was met by a page who escorted her inside.

Daniel climbed back into the Bentley. He turned his head to back out and found himself in the auditorium. Truth was there.   "I hate when you do that," he said to her.

"Oh well."

"Oh well? That's it?" Truth grinned. "I'm so proud of you."

"Yeah, I'm a real hero all right. Schmuck is more like it."

"What's a schmuck?"

"I think it's a Jewish dummy."

"You are a hero. Liam and Lily have a life full of love, and Sister Helen will save many children. The world will enjoy happiness, so humans can live on her for a while longer."

"That's a little much, don't ya think? I'm one man who helped one person, maybe two. So now I'm a saint? I also only did it 'cause I had to. Think about that, pumpkin."

"That's all it takes—one soul helping another. And the fact is that you didn't want to do it but you did it anyway. That, pumpkin, is a hero. You made the most with the least."

"Whatever."

"What is the matter with you?"

"I killed people in my other life, so I got killed. Over, done. But it turns out I wasn't supposed to die. Supposedly I saved a life, so I got a second chance. That's great, and what do I gotta do? Give the woman I love to another man."

"You killed her in that life. Sorry we do rebirths; should we have checked with you first? You stopped her from ruining her life again. If she had, she would have gone with Pride. You stopped that."

171

"But I can't get her back."

"No, you can't."

"Why?"

"Because love put you and her together. As Nicky and Lisa, you had a life to share. You chose to take her life—a life that was not yours to take. So you lost the privilege of her loving you. You gave your life for another, that's true, so we decided to give you another chance. And so far you've been great."

"I just wanna be alone for a while. I need to take it all in. I made other people, other families, live with heartache, didn't I?"

"That was a lifetime ago. You're doing good now."

"I can't get over losing her. She said she still loves me."

"She also said she set you free. Let it go."

"Yo, you gotta admit it's a lot to absorb."

"I guess so."

"So can you let me be?"

The doors opened and Faith walked in. She shouted to Daniel, "Come on, sweetie. Time's a-wasting."

"What do you mean—go? I just got here. I wanna relax."

"You can relax when you're dead. So who knows when you can relax."

Daniel laughed. "You're very funny."

Truth stepped forward. "Enough. Get going, Daniel."

"Get going where?"

"You have a date with an angel."

THOMAS JOSEPH BECK

THOMAS JOSEPH BECK

Thomas Beck is the author of the thought-provoking, and often humorous, Without Wings series.

Discovering John Steinbeck's *Grapes of Wrath* in high school, Beck was inspired to become an author. While also embraced his culinary skills, he never gave up the idea of writing books that would inspire and also make people laugh.

The Without Wings series has been called an alternative spiritual allegory. The root themes of good vs. evil, salvation, and redemption, are explored with Beck's unique sense of wonder and humor.

Thomas Beck lives in Bentonville, Arkansas with his lovely wife, Elizabeth.

" I have been writing bad short stories and poetry for twenty years but this is finally my work worth publishing. Hope it inspires and makes you laugh!"- TJB

BOOKS IN THE WITHOUT WINGS SERIES
Book 1: To Save a Soul
Book 2: Gambling on a Soul
Book 3: To Blame a Soul

SoulWithoutWings.com

Made in the USA
Middletown, DE
14 February 2022

60974763R00099